TARA SIVEC and ANDI ARNDT

Edits by KD Robichaux
facebook.com/AuthorKDRobichaux

Interior Design by Paul Salvette, BB eBooks
bbebooksthailand.com

Prologue

"HELLO, EVERYONE! WELCOME to Heidi's Discount Erotica Podcast, episode number ten. I'm really sorry I haven't uploaded anything new lately, but I promise I've been reading all your comments. I've just been… going through a little something, and I needed some time. I'm going to do something different today, so I hope—" I jump in my seat as my mom bursts through my front door.

"Hi, honey! I brought you dinner. Let me just move some of this stuff out of the way," she says, sliding all my notes on my coffee table from in front of me.

"Mom! I'm in the middle of recording a podcast. Didn't you see the **Do not knock, ring doorbell, or disturb. Recording in process** sign on the front door?"

"Uff da! Of course I saw the sign. Obviously it wasn't meant for your mother. Especially when she brings you a tater tot hotdish. So, I was at the supermarket today and ran into Shirley. You remember Shirley—from church? She told me there was a sale on ground meat. Can you believe they marked it down to ninety-three cents a pound? So I got a few pounds of ground meat to put in the freezer in the garage, and then I remembered your dad told me we were out of those mini frozen pizzas he likes to eat during his Sunday afternoon poker games with the boys. I was in the frozen pizza aisle, and I saw they had frozen corn on sale. Now, you know I only like to get fresh corn from the Hastings Farm over on Wilson Road, but it's nice to have some put away in the freezer for the winter, and you just can't pass up such a good deal, so I grabbed ten bags. I went up and down the freezer section, looking for more good deals, and then I ran into Carrie. You remember Carrie—the one you used to work with at the school? She was so nice, asking how you were and what you were up to. I started telling her about the little show you've been doing and how proud we are of you, even if you talk about things on the show that I can never repeat in public. So, that's why I'm here!"

"That doesn't at all explain why you're here," I reply, still wondering how my mother can tell a story that long without seeming to take a single breath.

She huffs. "It's like you don't even listen to me, Heidi. Frozen tater tots were on sale. I know you get so busy when you work on this little recording thingy that you forget to eat, and I just thought it would be nice to bring something for all your fans to enjoy. Everyone likes my tater tot hotdish."

I give her a placating smile. "Mom, that's really very

sweet of you, but that's not how this works. First of all, I have a lot of listeners. One hotdish would not be able to feed them."

She waves her hand to dismiss my concerns. "It's fine. I have seven more tater tot hotdishes in the car. I'll just go out and get them. You should always have enough food to feed your guests. I can't believe you don't even have any Jell-O salad prepared or at least a cheese ball set out. I know you've been on a mission to find yourself, but that doesn't mean you should forget about your upbringing and all of the manners I taught you."

I stare at her blankly for a moment, and then proceed to try to explain. "Mom, I love you, but there won't be any guests in the house. This is all done on the computer and then put out on the internet for people to listen to whenever they want. My listeners don't come to my house to watch me record my podcast, so they don't need a hotdish, Jell-O salad, or cheese. These people don't live across the street or down the block. They live all over the place."

"I know of one particular listener who lives very close to you who might enjoy my tater tot hotdish." She purses her lips and raises one perfectly manicured eyebrow.

"We're not talking about him right now. I still haven't figured out how to fix that little problem, so that's going on the back burner right now," I murmur.

She rolls back the tinfoil on the tater tots, and I reach over and snag one with my fingers before she swats me. "Fine. Then what are you talking about on this podcast thingy you're recording tonight?"

"Well, since I have a bunch of new listeners, and some that have been with me for a while, I thought it would be nice to recap everything that's happened so they can get the full story, and not just my random podcast ramblings where I leave a bunch of stuff out. I'm going to start at the beginning and tell them everything. I think they deserve to know it all."

"So, you *will* be talking about a certain handsome gentleman who lives very close to you. Hold on, let me just pull up a chair and get comfy. I brought forks and plates so we don't even need to go into the kitchen to eat the tater tot hotdish." She opens the plastic grocery bag hanging from her arm.

I'm already shaking my head. "Mom, you can't be here while I record my podcast."

Her brow furrows. "And why not? I brought you a—"

"If you say tater tot hotdish one more time…."

She grabs the back of my rolling computer chair from in front of my desk and wheels it over to sit next to the coffee table, divvying out some of the cheesy deep fried potatoes onto two plates before setting one in front of me with a fork. "Just pretend like I'm not even here. Can you show me how to use the record a video thingy on my cell phone? I want to memorialize this and show

4

it to the ladies at church. My famous daughter, talking to all her fans. If someone calls in, can I answer the call and patch them through to you?"

It takes everything in me not to give myself a full-on facepalm. "It's not a live radio show, Mom. People don't call in. If you're going to sit there, you have to be quiet. I'm already going to have enough work to do editing out this whole conversation. And just so you know, since I'm going back to the beginning, I'm going to have to talk about dirty things, since you now know that's how this podcast basically started and why it's called Heidi's Discount Erotica."

She lifts her brow again. "How dirty are we talking?

"Episode six dirty," I reply.

She looks scandalized. "Oh, my. Was that the one where he put his—"

"Yes."

"And then he did that thing with his—"

"Yes."

"I might need a few more tater tot hotdishes to get through this. Just give me a signal when you get to the dirty parts. Wave your hands in the air or something just so I can brace myself."

I can't help but giggle. I love my mom, as crazy as she is. "I can't believe I'm doing this. Okay, let's try this again. Hello, everyone! Welcome to Heidi's Discount Erotica Podcast, episode number ten. I'm going to do something a little different today, so I hope you enjoy it.

I feel like I've left a lot of things out of my podcasts, and since you guys have all been so amazing throughout this entire process, I want to go back to the beginning and tell you everything. I want you to know why I, Heidi Larson, a former kindergarten teacher, decided to start recording podcasts reading the dirtiest parts I could find from erotic romance novels, how I found the perfect guy who appreciated everything about me, and how I screwed it all up."

"Do you have to say the word 'erotic' so much?" Mom asks through a mouthful.

I sigh, giving my mother a glare before beginning once again. "Heidi's Discount Erotica Podcast, episode ten, take three."

Chapter 1

Three months earlier...

CLOSING MY EYES, I take a deep, calming breath and enjoy the peaceful sounds of a beautiful, hot summer night in Waconia, Minnesota. Sitting in a chair on the front porch of my home after the long, stressful day I had, there's nothing more soothing than listening to the chirping of crickets, the low buzz of Cicadas, and a woman loudly announcing all the dirty things she'd like to do to my neighbor.

Wait, what?

"I'm not wearing any panties under this skirt, Brent. We should celebrate our first date by getting *completely* naked."

My eyes fly open and my heart starts beating erratically in my chest when her high-pitched, nasally voice interrupts my serenity.

I really love the street where I live, lined with adorable, bungalow-style houses on each side, but having everyone's houses so close together means it's easy to hear what your neighbors are saying when they're outside. Normally, I don't mind hearing Mrs. Peterson lovingly talk to her rosebushes because she believes it makes them grow and flourish, or Mr. Olson grumbling about his twelve-year-old lawnmower that never wants to start. Listening to them talk to themselves always makes me smile. But this? Oh my goodness. This isn't doing anything to help me stay relaxed.

"Why don't we go inside and you can introduce me to that impressive bulge in your pants I've been eying all night."

Oh jeez, who talks like this? Outside, on the sidewalk, where God and everyone can hear them no less?

I need to quietly get up from my chair, sneak back inside my house, and not eavesdrop on this conversation any further. As soon as I stand and the view of my neighbor's walkway that leads up to his house is no longer hindered by the large purple hydrangea bush right next to my porch, my feet suddenly become frozen in place when I see *him*.

Brent Miller. The sweetest, handsomest man I've ever met, with his short, dirty blond hair and piercing blue eyes. He bought the house next to mine a few months ago after relocating from California, and he's the main reason I've been spending so much time on my front porch lately, just so I can catch a glimpse of him.

Sometimes, when he's outside at the same time as me, he'll shout hello from his front yard and ask me how I am. A bunch of times, he's walked over and sat in the extra chair next to mine on my front porch and asked me about my day, or had me tell him about the other people who live on our street, since he hasn't had a chance to meet them all yet. Once in a while, if he's in a hurry, he just lifts his hand with a wave and a smile before disappearing inside his house. I live for those moments where his attention is on me. For those few seconds or minutes where my heart beats faster and I try to come up with something clever or funny to say just to see the dimples in his cheeks when he smiles.

With the bright glow of the street lamp by the side-walk in front of Brent's house, I can see the corner of his mouth tip up into a half smile as he looks at the woman standing in front of him, and a rush of jealously shoots through me.

"I've been thinking about putting your cock in my mouth all through dinner."

This woman's brazen words and the way she presses her body flush up against Brent right in the middle of his yard forces a gasping squeak out of me. My hand flies up to my mouth to try to muffle the noise, but it's too late. Brent's eyes swing in my direction, and I do what any sane, twenty-five-year-old woman would do when she's spying on the man she has a massive crush on. I duck down behind the hydrangeas as fast as possible before he can see me. Unfortunately, I move too quickly and lose my footing on the edge of my concrete front porch, which I now regret never installing a railing around the edge of. My body topples down the two feet between the porch and the ground, getting scraped by hydrangea branches as I go. I land on my shoulder, letting out a quiet, pain-filled "*oof!*" as I flop into a heap under the shrubbery.

"I had a nice time tonight, Laura, but I need to be up early for work tomorrow morning."

Laura! I knew that voice sounded familiar.

Laura Newberg, with perfect, thick blonde hair, and perfect long legs, who always made fun of me in elementary school because I wore glasses, who laughed at the colorful tights I wore under my dresses regardless of the temperature, and who always called me "cute." But not in a nice way. In a "Well, aren't you just *cute*" way, where it sounds condescending, like I'm a puppy. Perfect, beautiful Laura Newberg, who always introduced herself as, "Laura, with an a-u", like there was any other way to spell Laura.

While I hold my body perfectly still in the fetal position on the ground, Brent's deep, raspy voice travels across our two yards and makes me forget all about the pain and embarrassment of falling off my porch and the misery I felt when he smiled at his date. Especially since he seems to be giving Laura with an a-u the brushoff as politely as he can.

"Are you sure? I could make the late night worth your while. Not to brag or anything, but I've gotten a lot of compliments on my blowjob skills."

Laura practically purrs these words, and my mouth drops open in shock that she would have the nerve to say something so forward to a man on their first date. I wouldn't even say that to a man on our twentieth date. Or our eight-hundredth. Or our fiftieth wedding anniversary.

I realize I don't know Brent all that well, but I cannot believe he would actually take someone like Laura on a date. Here I thought finding out earlier today that I've been laid off as a kindergarten teacher because of budget cuts was the worst thing that could happen to me. Instead, the sadness and dread sitting like a rock in my stomach right now is because I'm wondering if *this* is the type of woman Brent is attracted to. I've never been able to even ask a man to kiss me before. Just the idea of vocalizing something like that makes me break out in a cold sweat. I can't imagine *thinking* the things Laura has said in the middle of Brent's yard, let alone saying them out loud.

Hugging my knees to my chest, I listen to Brent repeat that he had a nice time with her at dinner, but that he really needs to get to bed early, and asking for a raincheck. A *raincheck!* Which means he definitely liked the things Laura said she wanted to do to him and wouldn't mind taking her up on her offer another time when he doesn't have to be up so early in the morning. Closing my eyes, I can picture those adorable dimples in his cheeks as he smiles down at her, and it makes me a little nauseous. A few seconds later, I hear the heels of her shoes clicking against the sidewalk, followed by the slam of a door, and the start of a car engine. I finally relax a little when the sound of her car driving away fills the night, and I unwrap my arms from around my legs, rolling over to push myself up from the ground.

"You okay in there, Heidi?"

My body jolts when I hear Brent's voice right on the other side of the hydrangeas, and once again, I freeze, still partially crouched down behind the bush.

Oh no! Oh jeez!

"You betcha!" I shout through the leaves and branches in a loud chipper voice, thankful he can't see my face redden in complete mortification. "Thought I saw a few dead flowers on the hydrangea bush and I wanted to get rid of them, because you should always prune your bushes!"

Son of a nutcracker, Heidi! Stop talking!

"Need any help in there?" Brent asks, the laughter in his voice coming through loud and clear.

"Nope, nope. I'm good, but thank you for asking. Just gonna finish up and then head on inside. Boy, is it hot out here tonight or what? I know you're from California and probably used to the heat, but just wait. Minnesotans like to say we have four seasons: Winter, More Winter, Still More Winter, and That One Day of Summer," I giggle uncomfortably.

I roll my eyes at myself, knowing I sound like a complete idiot, but there's nothing I can do to stop it. It's not like I can just ignore him or be short with him when he's asking me questions. I was raised to never be rude to anyone, even if you're hiding in a bush after spying on your crush, and that crush *knows* you were spying on him, and you're too embarrassed to remove yourself from the bush, because he just went on a date with perfect, dirty-talking Malibu Barbie, and your long, wavy black hair that you pulled up into a high ponytail looked kind of nice when you got home from work earlier, but it's now all askew and looks like a rat's nest with leaves stuck in it.

"It's definitely pretty humid out here tonight. You sure you're okay?" Brent asks again in a kind voice that makes me want to melt into a puddle of goo.

I quickly start grabbing at leaves and branches, the entire bush shaking and swaying as I pluck whatever I can get my hands on just to try and prove that I was, in fact, out here pruning my hydrangeas at 10:00 at night.

"Yep! I'm super. Thanks for asking! You should probably go on inside now, since you have to get up early for work tomorrow."

I hear Brent chuckle softly, and I can't stop the low groan that comes out of my mouth, realizing I just completely screwed up any attempt to make him believe I was not actually listening to his conversation with Laura. I should probably pay attention to my mother more often when she says, *"Liars never prosper."*

"Okay, well, I'll leave you to your pruning. Have a good night, Heidi."

My hands immediately stop their manic plucking of hydrangea leaves when I hear my name come out of his mouth again, all soft and sweet. I clamp my lips closed as tightly as possible while I listen to him walk away, so I don't do anything else embarrassing like sigh loudly or giggle again.

Spreading a few of the branches apart with my hands, I watch Brent walk back over to his yard, jog up the stairs of his front porch, and disappear inside his house.

One of these days, I'm going to figure out how to talk to that man without making a fool of myself. As soon as I figure out what in the world I'm going to do about getting a new job before my mother finds out and marches into the principal's office with fifteen dozen of her famous brown butter sugar cookie bars to try to guilt him into giving me my job back, that's going to be my top priority.

Chapter 2

"**D**ID YOU TRY Southview Elementary?" my mother questions, as we stand out on the front lawn of our church after Sunday service.

The rest of the congregation is gathered in small groups all around us, chatting about life and the sermon we heard today, which coincidentally was about picking yourself back up when you've been knocked down.

"Yes," I reply, trying to keep the exasperation out of my voice.

"Bayview?"

"Yes."

"Laketown?"

"Yes. And before you even ask, I checked every elementary school within a fifty-mile radius. There's a hiring freeze in schools all over the state of Minnesota right now. No one is hiring new teachers, especially ones without tenure," I remind her.

We've already had this discussion at least ten times in the last week since I was let go from my teaching position at Trinity Lutheran Elementary. My phone was ringing off the hook before I could even pull all of the hydrangea leaves out of my hair when I scurried back into my house after my disastrous interaction with Brent. As much as I would have liked to keep this news from her for as long as I could, not only was it impossible in this small town we live in where everyone knows everyone else's business, but it was also hopeless. My mother is a retired kindergarten teacher from Trinity Lutheran. She still keeps in touch with every single teacher employed there and also has a standing lunch date every month with the vice principal, the secretary, and the guidance counselor. My father plays poker with the principal and my former boss of Trinity Lutheran. The same Trinity Lutheran whose lawn we are currently standing on, where we attend church every Sunday.

"Did you try St. Joseph Catholic School?"

"Oh, hey now, Margie!" My mother scoffs at my aunt, who turns around to join our conversation after saying hello to one of her neighbors. "We're Lutheran. We don't work in Catholic schools. Ever heard of the Reformation?"

"Fine. Then who gives a rat's patootie what she does, Peggy? Let the poor girl take some time off and figure out what she wants to do with her life. There's no rule that says she even has to be a teacher," Aunt Margie states.

Right about now, I'd love to give my aunt a hug and tell her how much I love her, but going by how red my mother's face is getting, I'm just going to stand here watching their conversation like I'm at a tennis match, with my head bouncing back and forth between them. My aunt and my mother are like two sides of the same coin and often get mistaken for twins. They're both slim and stand around 5'4", and both go to the same hair dresser like clockwork every six weeks to get rid of the grays and clean up the ends of their dark brown, chin-length bobs. The only difference between them is my Aunt Margie's mouth. She tends to be a little more… colorful than my mother. She's also always on my side, no matter what the subject matter may be.

"Heidi is a teacher. Heidi will *always* be a teacher. It's in her blood. It's what she was always meant to do," Mom says passionately. "It's bad enough she's still single and hasn't given me any grandbabies yet. When I was her age, I already had tenure and had been happily married to her father for seven years, God rest his soul."

"Dad's not dead," I interject quietly.

"He will be if he doesn't convince Lou to give you your job back."

The three of us turn and look behind me where my dad is currently talking to his poker buddy and my former boss, Principal Lou Shephard.

My mom lets out a sigh of frustration when the two of them throw their heads back and laugh, clearly not having a heated discussion about my teaching position like she had hoped. I can't help but feel a little happy that my dad isn't on the same crusade my mother is to get me my job back. I keep that thought to myself as I turn back around, and my aunt and mother continue with their argument about my future employment.

From the moment I could talk, whenever anyone asked me what I wanted to be when I grew up, I would tell them I wanted be a teacher just like my mother. She'd be standing right there beaming the whole time, and it wasn't until later that I wondered if that was the real reason I gave the answer I always did. By then, I'd gotten my degree in elementary education, and after student teaching and getting my certifications, I immediately went to work at the same place where my mother had spent thirty years molding the minds of five-and-six-year-olds. I don't even know when things changed, really. All I know is that within the last six months or so, every morning when I got up to get ready for work, I did it with dread. I dragged my feet and I grumbled and moaned through my morning routine, pasting on a fake smile as soon as I walked through the school doors. Don't get me wrong; I love children. I *adore* them. I want to have my own children someday in the distant future. But being in charge of other people's children for eight hours a day just didn't excite me as much as I thought it would. Dealing with angry parents who yelled at you because they thought you weren't doing enough, yelled at you because they thought you were doing too much, or just yelled at you because they had no one else to yell at when their son or daughter was struggling in school wasn't what I signed up for. Neither were the politics or the gossip or the stress of not being allowed as much creative freedom as I wanted, since every decision I made on what to teach and how I taught it had to be approved by someone else.

I wasn't passionate about my work, and that made me sad. Shouldn't you love what you do when you spend more time at work than you do at home with friends and family? I spent four years going to school, another year getting certified, and then taught on my own for two years. And I can't remember one single moment during that time that I was absolutely confident this was what I was meant to do. So many of my childhood memories are filled with my mom talking about her day at work. The excitement on her face, the animation of her entire body as she told us about a particular lesson she was working on, her hands waving around while she bounced on the balls of her feet. I wanted that for myself. I wanted to be *excited*.

But then I feel guilty when I think about my father. He worked as an electrician for more than thirty years. I know he didn't particularly love his job. There were no animated conversations at the dinner table about a light fixture he installed. But he still went to work every day. He showed up without complaint no matter how much he might have hated his job, because that's what his generation was taught. You went to work so you could pay your bills, put food on the table, and keep a roof over your family's heads. It's what *I* was taught. And here I stand, completely rejecting the morals they instilled in me.

I am the absolute worst.

"When I was Heidi's age, I was footloose and fancy free," Aunt Margie sighs with a wistful smile, pulling me out of my thoughts. "She's young, she's smart, and she's got some money saved to keep her afloat for a while until she figures out what she wants to do. She doesn't need to be married and popping out babies. If I had her adorable face and cute little figure, I would have kissed a lot more handsome men than I did back in the day before I settled down with Harold; mark my words. As soon as I met Harold, I had to hang up my *necking in the backseat of the car* shoes."

"Shush now, Margie! We don't talk about that," my mom scolds, quickly looking around to make sure no one heard.

Aunt Margie leans in close to my ear and whispers, "It's true. I had *necking in the backseat of the car* shoes. They were red leather platform wedges and they drove the men wild, let me tell you. I still have them in my closet if you want them."

I feel my cheeks blush and I laugh uncomfortably, shaking my head at her.

Then I think about Laura Newberg and the red stilettos she had on the night she went on her date with Brent and I wonder if I should take my aunt up on her offer. My mother interjects before I can even gather up the nerve to maybe ask her what size the shoes are.

"Can we please get back to discussing the important matter at hand? Heidi needs a job. A teaching job. She can't just be unemployed. That's not how we raised her. Children need to be self-sufficient. She needs to earn her keep by making an honest living, and there's nothing more honest than being a teacher. What are we going to do about this, Margie?"

I hate that everyone is always talking around me when I'm standing right here. Being my parents' only child, I've always felt the pressure of being the perfect daughter and never straying from the path that made them happy. My job gave my mother something to brag about to her friends. It put a big smile on my father's face whenever he'd ask me about my lesson plans. But ever since I started feeling so *blah* about my job as a teacher, I wondered what my life would be like right now if I'd thought more about what made *me* happy when I planned out my future. Would I stop letting people talk about me like I'm not even here? Would I have told Brent by now that I have a crush on him? I doubt I'd be so bold as to mention the... you know... *thing* in his pants or... what I wanted to... *do* with it, but who knows? If I would have spoken up years ago, told my parents that I wasn't sure if being a teacher was the right path for me to take, who knows what kind of a woman

I'd be right now? Well, now it's time for me to take charge of my own destiny. I already took the first step of making a decision without consulting my mother about it first. Now it's time to take the second. Telling her about it.

"Mom, I need to—"

"I haven't made Lou my tuna hotdish yet. Maybe that's the problem," she muses.

"I actually have a—"

"If you're going to make him anything, make him your lutefisk with bacon," Aunt Margie adds, interrupting me again. "That's how I always get Harold to say yes to anything,"

"There's no need to—"

"You remember Sherry, from high school? Her daughter, Melanie, the poor thing who had scoliosis and trouble pronouncing her Rs. She became a big shot lawyer and moved to New York. Broke Sherry's heart, it did," my mother says with a shake of her head, resting her hand over her heart. "She moved back to Waconia a few months ago. Lives in that big house out on Hilliard Road with her husband who started some sort of investment company. You remember that house, the one with the white siding and blue shutters with the koi pond and fountain in front?"

Aunt Margie makes the "speed it up" motion with her hands, something I've always wanted to do when my mother goes on one of her long-winded tangents before she finally gets to the point of her story.

"Anyhoo, I ran into Melanie at the grocery store the other day after I stopped by the doctor to get a refill on my bursitis medication. There was construction on County Road 10, so I had to take 102nd Street to Little Avenue. She's got the most adorable little boy named Carter who she just put in Sunday school, so I'll just have a little chat with Pastor Bob and that will fix everything."

"Cheese and rice, Peggy, how will that fix anything?" Aunt Margie asks with a roll of her eyes that makes me struggle to contain my laughter.

"We're going to need another Sunday school teacher, Margie. Pay attention! It's not a paying job, but at least it will keep Heidi's teaching skills sharp. I'll just go over there right now and put the bug in his ear and get the ball rolling," my mother states, starting to turn away from us.

Before I lose my nerve, my hand shoots out and I wrap it around her arm, stopping her from walking over to our pastor.

"You don't have to talk to Pastor Bob or make anyone food, because I already have a job interview for tomorrow that I'm really excited about, and it's not a teaching job, but it pays pretty well, and there's no need to worry, because everything will be fine!" I gasp for air.

"Oh, Heidi, that's wonderful news. See, Peggy? I told you she was a smart girl," Aunt Margie smiles, wrapping her arm around my shoulders and giving me a tight squeeze.

"What job interview? Where is it? What will you be doing? Why didn't you tell me about this? Is it safe? Who will you be working for? What do you mean it's not a teaching job?" Mom asks rapid fire in a panic.

"It's a newer company in Eden Prairie and they need an administrative assistant. I saw the ad in the paper, I sent them an email, and they called me right away for an interview," I tell her, not wanting to give her too many more details in case she gets it in her head that she should go down there with a basket full of baked goods.

"Okay, but what do they do there? Can you work your way up to a teaching position?"

"Give it a rest, Peggy. Our girl has a job interview and she's going to knock them dead, aren't-cha, kiddo?" Aunt Margie encourages.

"I certainly hope so," I reply as butterflies start flapping around in my stomach when I think about tomorrow.

The only thing I know about this company is that it's called EdenMedia, and they do some sort of audio recordings there. It's something new and exciting, and it's not teaching, which scares me a little bit, but this is what I want. Something different. Something out of my comfort zone that will help me decide what I want to do with the rest of my life if I'm not going to be a teacher. And it's a job my mother has no part in helping me get, which makes it all the more enticing.

"Call me when you're on your way, and then call me as soon as the interview is over so I know you're okay," my mother demands. "And give me the address, and the name of the owner. I'll drop off a pan of my lemon bars tomorrow afternoon."

Chapter 3

"**Y**OU'RE HIRED."

I blink rapidly and my mouth drops open in shock when Jessica, the hugely pregnant woman standing next to me behind the receptionist desk of EdenMedia, winces and rubs her hand over her belly.

Our interview has only lasted five minutes, where she quickly listed off all of the things they were looking for in an administrative assistant, and the only question she asked me was, "Do you think you can handle all that?"

"Oh, jeez, are you okay?"

She takes a few deep breaths as the pain leaves her face and she shoots me a huge smile. "You betcha! Just some Braxton Hicks contractions. I no longer have ankles; I wouldn't be able to see them even if I did. My back hurts, I'm tired all the time, and my husband told me if I didn't start my maternity leave now and get some rest before the baby comes, he'd hide my car keys and stop stocking the freezer with mint chocolate chip ice cream. And he'd do it, believe you me."

I return her smile, not really knowing what to say to

that, since I've never been pregnant and mint chocolate chip ice cream isn't my favorite. Jessica leans down with a groan and grabs her purse from the bottom drawer of the desk, sliding the strap over her shoulder.

"So, like I said, you're hired. You only really need organizational skills to do this job, and since you were a teacher, I'm sure you've got those in spades. You seem sweet, you've got a great smile, and you dress professionally. Everyone here is super nice, and they'll help you out if you have any questions," she explains, moving around the desk toward a long hallway.

She waves to me with her hand, indicating I should follow her, and I quickly scramble around the desk to catch up to her.

"I'll just show you around really quick and introduce you to some people before I head out. You said over email you're able to start immediately. You'll be fine sticking around for the next couple hours, right?" she asks as we pass by a few dark, empty offices.

"Um, sure," I tell her, not exactly sure I'm sure, but I don't want to be rude and tell her I'd much rather start *after* I've gotten the lay of the land and actually know what I'm doing.

EdenMedia is located in an office park where it's one long, single story building filled with a bunch of different businesses that all share the same parking lot. My mother and a bunch of her friends all go to the dentist that is located right next door, which should ease her fears about where I'm going to be working and whether or not it's safe.

"Don't worry; there's not much going on today aside from one recording in progress. You'll just need to answer phones and check on the narrator who's here today. See if he needs anything to eat or drink, that sort of thing," Jessica explains as we get to the end of the hallway and turn a corner, stopping right in front of a huge glass window.

Directly in front of the window, I see a man with his back to us, sitting behind a computer. On the table next to the computer is a giant, flat, square piece of equipment lined with all sorts of buttons and switches. In front of the man and his table of electronics is yet another large window that separates him from a smaller room, where I see a man perched on the edge of a stool, wearing a pair of headphones and speaking into a microphone.

"Right here in front of us is Dave. Dave is one of our producers. The computer you see in front of him is what we refer to as DAW, or Digital Audio Workstation. The sound levels on the DAW are all set up at the very beginning of a recording, and they're pretty much left alone so the audio quality is consistent for that specific project," Jessica explains. "The man in the recording booth with the headphones is narrator Steve Reynolds."

I watch as Dave lounges back in his chair with his hands clasped behind his head, staring at the DAW and what looks to be sound waves floating across it.

"What are they recording right now?" I ask as Jessica moves toward the door leading to where Dave is sitting.

"A romance novel," she says with a shrug as she knocks lightly on the window.

Romances? I love romances!

I have two bookshelves in my living room filled to the brim with romance novels. My mother got me hooked a few years ago on a series of Amish love stories. That might not sound very exciting to some, but they are so beautiful and have such amazing storylines. What if I got to see one of those books being made into an audiobook? I'll have no other choice but to see if my mother can stop by and watch once she finds this out.

Dave glances over his shoulder and smiles at Jessica, waving her into the room. I quickly follow behind her as she opens the door, waiting for me to move inside the room before she closes it behind me.

"Steve, let's break for a few seconds and redo that last line. We need to understand just how much he wants this to happen. I'd like you to really emphasize the word *pump* this next time as well," Dave speaks into a microphone right in front of him before swiveling around in his chair to face us.

This is amazing! I wonder what the character in this book wants to happen. I bet this is an Amish romance if they're talking about pumping something. Must be pumping water from a well during this scene. Oh, my mother is going to be absolutely beside herself!

I watch Steve remove his headphones from inside the recording booth and take a drink from a bottle of water perched on a second stool right next to him before I move my eyes to Dave and smile at him.

"Dave, this is Heidi Larson. She's going to be my replacement. Heidi, this is Dave Simpson, the best producer we have," Jessica introduces as I hold out my hand for Dave to shake.

"Awww, jeez, Jessica, don't make me blush. It's good to meet-cha, Heidi." He laughs before dropping my hand. "So, I guess Brian threatened your mint chocolate chip supply again, did he?"

"You know it." Jessica nods. "You guys will be in good hands with Heidi. She used to be a teacher, so she'll be able to keep you crazy kids in line."

"That sounds great. Feel free to let me know if you have any questions, Heidi. There aren't too many people here today, but you'll be able to meet everyone else tomorrow. They're all gonna be real glad to have you on board. Don't you worry," he reassures me.

"I actually have a question. What book are you recording right now? I'm an avid reader, and so is my mother. Romances are our favorite, and she will just *die* if you're recording for an author we've read before. This is so exciting. She's going to love it when I tell her about this."

"Instead of telling you, how about we show you?

Steve is recording a new romance novel that's publishing next month," Dave replies as he turns away from us, presses a button, and leans forward to speak into his microphone.

Oooh! A new book we haven't even read yet!

"Steve, let's take it from the top of page one-hundred-and-four, paragraph two."

Dave reaches over and flips a switch on the table, and all of a sudden, I can hear Steve clear his throat through a speaker mounted on the wall right next to Jessica.

I can't stop the giddy excitement that courses through me knowing I'm about to hear someone read lines from a book that hasn't even been published yet. Any second thoughts I had about taking this job disappear in an instant as I watch Steve slide his headphones back on and get close to his microphone.

"See that stand in front of Steve?" Dave asks, keeping his eyes glued to his computer screen. "It's got an iPad resting on it with the book's manuscript pulled up. He did a quick read-through of the book once and made some notes on the iPad about scene changes, who's talking, major events, those sorts of things."

"He only read the book once, and now he has to act out the entire thing?" I ask in astonishment.

"They're lucky if they even get to read it once. Sometimes, when they walk into the recording booth, that's the first time they've seen the book," Jessica tells me.

"Don't tell the poor girl all of our horror stories on her first day or she'll never come back tomorrow." Dave laughs.

I hear Steve clear his throat a few more times and take another sip of water. He glances through his window at Dave, who points at him and nods, indicating Steve can go ahead and start whenever he's ready. My heart starts beating even faster in my chest at just how exciting this whole process will be to watch and learn more about. I was dreading calling my mother when I left here today, and now I can't wait.

"Testing, testing... are the sound levels still good?"

The richness of Steve's voice through the speakers makes goose bumps break out on my arms. There's no other way to describe it other than warm and luxurious. He's only spoken a total of eight words and I already know I'd enjoy listening to anything he'd want to read to me.

And then, Steve starts reading from the iPad.

"She takes the swollen head of my cock deep into her wet, warm mouth. So deep it touches the back of her throat. I groan in pleasure when she tightly wraps her hand around my manhood and begins pumping her fist up and down my length. *Pump, pump, pump.* My cock throbs and jerks in her hand as her head bobs up and down on my stiff rod, and I know I'm going to come harder than I ever have in my life with how hard she sucks on me."

Oh, jeez! Oh, holy mother of pearl, what is happening right now? Why is no one screaming? Why is Jessica just standing here next to me with a smile on her face? Does she not hear the words Steve is saying? Why is Steve saying the word... pump... like that? What kind of a romance novel is this?

"Perfect!" Dave shouts into his microphone. "That was much better than the last time. You really had the passion and heat down pat with this one. I could actually *feel* the desire in your voice. Heidi, what do you think? Could you feel the desire? Did it sound hot enough?"

Oh, it's definitely hot in here, all right. I think I need to stick my head into a bucket of ice right about now.

"It was... super!" I tell him with an uncomfortable giggle, wondering if it would be rude to turn and run out of this room as fast as possible before Steve says the word *pump* again. Or any of those other words that will now require me to rinse out my ears with bleach. Oh jeez, I know I wanted something new and exciting in my life, but I don't know if I can handle this much exhilaration. I know my *mother* won't be able to handle it.

Oh no, my mother! What in the world am I supposed to tell her about this job?

"This book is going to be huge," Jessica informs me. "It's called *Falling for my Secretary* by Penelope Sharp. Her first book, *Sleeping with my Secretary*, was an instant bestseller. She's already been dubbed the queen of erotic romance novels and popularized a new sub-genre called Office Romantica. Lots of hot sex scenes on desks and stuff like that. Her first book is how I got pregnant." Jessica chuckles, rubbing her hand over her belly. "I've got a few copies of the first one and an advance copy of the one we're recording now in the lower, left-hand drawer of the front desk. Make sure you take them home. You'll love them."

I'm pretty sure I will not love them. And I'm one hundred percent positive I will never, ever open that lower, left-hand drawer.

"Oh, I almost forgot. Eric cleaned out one of the cabinets filled with old equipment and left it on the floor under your desk," Dave tells Jessica as he fiddles with some buttons. "Can you take it out to the trash dumpster on your way out?"

"I'll do it!" I shout, raising my hand like one of my former students and hoping the dumpster is in Egypt.

"That would be great, Heidi. It's just some old pod-cast equipment we don't need anymore. Trash it, take it home, or do whatever you want with it. I better get back to work. We need to have this audiobook finished in three days," Dave says, looking back over his shoulder and giving me a thumbs-up. "See you tomorrow!"

I don't even know how Dave can say the word *book* with a straight face. Can this type of story even be classified as a book? I'm not completely oblivious. I've seen these types of books in the romance section of the bookstore, and I've walked by them as quickly as possible with their muscled, shirtless men covers and suggestive titles. I'm not one to judge people who like to read that sort of thing, but it's just not my cup of tea. I want something with a little more substance. Something with an actual storyline. Something a little more… tame. Some light kissing and then a lovely fade-to-black scene and not so in your face about what's going on behind closed doors. Aunt Margie calls them Mommy P-O-R-N. Every time she says that word, my mother shushes her.

As Jessica and I exit the room and make our way back down the hall to the reception area, I wonder how hard it would be for me to change my name and move to another country. That's probably the only thing that will save me from my mother when she finds out what they do here at EdenMedia. I'm certain she won't be bragging to any of her friends that I'm now an administrative assistant at a place that records… *dirty books.*

Chapter 4

"I'LL JUST QUIT. I'll call Jessica in a little while and I'll tell her I'm sorry but this job isn't a good fit for me," I whisper to myself as I pull the box out of my backseat.

I let out a sigh and shake my head at myself. I'm not a quitter. I've never quit anything in my life, even if it was horrible and I hated every minute of it. Like ballet classes when I was seven, because my mom thought it would be good for me to learn to be graceful. I stuck with it for an entire year, even though I have two left feet and was constantly knocking other girls down or smacking them in the face with my flailing arms and legs.

Or volleyball in middle school, because my dad thought being an athlete was a great way for me to learn teamwork. I couldn't hit the broadside of a barn, let alone a small, white ball that constantly came flying at my face at an unreasonable speed. I kept at it until high school, even though I suffered through one broken nose, two sprained wrists, and the embarrassment that I was the only girl on the team who never managed to get a serve over the net.

And then you have every blind date my mother has ever set me up on over the years. Although I wouldn't exactly call them "blind dates," since in this town you pretty much have to check with your grandmother before going on a date to make sure you aren't in some way related to the other person. No one I've ever dated has been a stranger. We all grew up together, we all went to school together, and everyone knows *someone* who is related to someone else. I never complained about these dates she set up for me, never got up and walked out on my date, even though I was tempted to several times. I dutifully sat through each and every meal, movie, trip for ice cream, and one disastrous Sunday afternoon of ice fishing where I was stuck out in the middle of the lake for hours with Jasper Reynolds, who always pulled my hair in kindergarten, and did nothing on our date but talk about how much he loves his mother and how, when he gets married, he'd continue living in her basement because he could never go a day without her meatloaf.

And let's not forget the whole teacher thing. I was actually pretty good at that though. I would never have quit my teaching job, no matter how much I didn't like it. That's just not what I was brought up to do, which means no matter how uncomfortable working at EdenMedia is, I know I have to stick with it. I do have some money set aside that could tide me over for a little while, but I can't just *not* work. What would I do, sit home all day staring out the window, hoping for a glimpse of Brent?

Actually, that doesn't sound like a bad idea.

Closing the back door of my car with a bump of my hip, I cradle the box of equipment tightly to my chest as I turn around, coming to an abrupt halt when I glance over at my neighbor's front yard.

Speaking of the handsome devil…. Wait, not a devil. He's not evil. He's not bad. He's perfect and wonderful and sweet and—

Brent stands up from a bent-over position where he was pulling weeds around the flower beds in front of his porch and stretches his arms high above his head, arching his back and twisting and turning at the waist to work the kinks out.

I'm frozen in place as I stand here blatantly staring at his shirtless torso. Under normal circumstances, I would have quickly looked away and ran into my house, but something about spending time with people who read dirty things into a microphone for a living—and were being told to put more *feeling* into those dirty things—seems to have altered my brain. And now all I can hear is Narrator Steve in my head with his deep, soothing voice.

"Brent's muscular body glistens with sweat after a hard evening of working on his flower beds. His faded jeans rest low on his narrow hips, showcasing the indents in his waist. My tongue darts out, wetting my parched lips as I wonder what his skin would taste like."

The box of equipment slips from my grasp and tumbles to the ground before I can even attempt to stop it. I knew I should have parked in the alley garage behind my house, but it was just easier to park along the curb in front so I didn't have to carry this box so far.

Why in the world didn't I throw this stuff in the dumpster like I was told?

I was so busy running as fast as I could out of EdenMedia at the end of the day that I shoved this stupid box into my backseat, figuring I'd just toss it when I got home. Now this box is going to be the death of me.

Brent's arms drop back down to his sides, and he jogs over to me when he hears the commotion of the box smacking the ground and everything spilling out of it at my feet, including...

Oh no! Please, God, no!

Ducking my head to hide the blush I feel heating my cheeks, I quickly squat down and try to shove everything back into the box before he gets to me, particularly the book Jessica must have shoved in there when I wasn't looking. A half-naked man, similar to the one heading right for me, smirks up at me from the cover of that stupid thing, and my arm darts out to grab it right as Brent gets to it first.

I watch in complete mortification as he bends over and grabs the book, and then I do everything I can to avoid eye contact. I finish shoving the cords, microphone, and other odds and ends back into the box and stand, hugging it to my body and keeping my downcast eyes on the box like it's filled with the most interesting things I've ever seen.

Don't look at his bare chest, don't look at his bare chest...

"*Sleeping with my Secretary,*" Brent muses as he flips the book over in his hands and studies the back cover. "Interesting reading you've got here."

Where is a giant hole in the ground that will open and swallow you up when you need it?

"It's not mine!" I blurt, finally lifting my head to stare at a spot over his shoulder, refusing to look anywhere between his head and the waist of his jeans for fear that Narrator Steve will start another commentary in my brain. "It's research for my new job at EdenMedia I started today. I was thinking about quitting, but I'm not a quitter, and Jessica put that book in this box from a drawer at the office that I'm now referring to as the Garden of Eden Drawer, because it's filled with temptation that will send me straight to H-E-double hockey sticks."

Oh jeez. Not only am I rambling; I sound like a person trying to sell door-to-door religion. What is wrong with me?

Brent chuckles, and the sound of it does all sorts of things to me that are appropriate for the book he's still holding in his hand, but not appropriate for sidewalk chitchat.

A few hours at EdenMedia and I've already been tainted,

getting all tingly when a man laughs. By this time next week, I'll probably be selling my body on a street corner and my mother will have disowned me.

"*'She wants him, in a way she's never wanted a man before,'*" Brent reads aloud from the back cover of the book. "*He lights a fire inside her she knows will never be extinguished, no matter how many times he bends her over his desk and takes everything she has to give.'* Wow. Sounds like fun research."

I giggle uncomfortably, still waiting for a hole in the ground to open up. Or maybe a time machine that will magically transport me back to EdenMedia, where I could stop Jessica from shoving that book from her drawer of sin into my box.

Brent sets the book on top of the equipment, and since I'd rather look anywhere but at that thing, my eyes move to his face and the heart-stopping smile he's aiming in my direction. There's a smudge of dirt on one of his cheeks, and Steve is back before I can stop him.

"*My hands itch to reach out and brush the dirt off his cheek, wondering what the stubble on his face would feel like against my palm.*"

I shake my head to get stupid Steve out of there, mentally telling him to go stand in a corner and think about what he's done.

"Well, I should probably get back to my weeds so I can finish while there's still some daylight left," Brent tells me, pointing his thumb over his shoulder toward his yard. "Have fun with your research."

Just the thought of him knowing I have this book in my possession and think I would even entertain the idea of going inside my house and reading it makes my scalp all itchy, and I almost drop the box in my arms again when my palms start to sweat.

"Oh, I'm just going to throw this whole box away. No research needed. Nothing but junk here. I might even light a fire out back and burn the whole thing. I don't have a fire pit, but I'm sure it's fine and I won't light my entire yard on fire." I laugh uncomfortably.

"Looks like you've got some nice equipment in there. Podcast stuff, right?" he asks, leaning closer to me and peering into the box. "I have a friend who records a podcast. It looks like outdated stuff, but you could probably still get it to work."

"I don't think anyone would want to listen to me talking to myself. What would I even talk about? My life isn't exciting or interesting enough for something like that," I reply quietly, looking down at myself.

I'm wearing a dress with yellow pencils on it, for goodness sake. My entire closet is filled with dresses covered in the alphabet, apples, and other kid-friendly designs that were appropriate to wear to school. My thoughts immediately turn to Laura and all the skin she was showing on her date with Brent, and how *she* wouldn't have any problems working at EdenMedia. Now, I just feel like a child standing next to a man who is out of my league and attracted to women who don't get embarrassed just by having a dirty book in her general vicinity.

"I think you're pretty interesting. You could talk about your new job," Brent suggests with a shrug, giving me a wink before he turns and starts walking back over to his yard.

I'm so busy being shocked by the fact that he thinks I'm interesting *and* that he winked at me that I never take my eyes off him as he walks away. I watch the muscles in his back ripple as his arms swing down by his sides. I don't realize I'm still standing on the sidewalk next to my car, watching Brent start pulling weeds again, until a car door slams a few houses down, making me jump and scurry up the walkway into my house.

Yep. It's official. EdenMedia has corrupted me. I don't know whether to be worried about it or look forward to what the future might bring.

As soon as I get inside my house and set the box on top of the kitchen table, my cell phone starts buzzing with an incoming call. When I pull it out of the front pocket of my dress and see I have seven missed calls from my mother, I'm thankful I had the foresight to pick up wine the other day when I was at the store.

Nothing bad ever happens when a woman is contemplating her entire existence and where she went wrong, home alone with a brand new box of wine chilling in her fridge and a dirty romance novel she's afraid to even touch, let alone read, which is suddenly calling her name after she heard her extremely attractive neighbor read the blurb on the back cover.

Said no one ever.

Chapter 5

Heidi's Podcast, Episode 1

"OKAY. UH, IS this thing even on? How do I know if it's on? Oh my God. This is so stupid. I'm gonna have the biggest headache in the morning, but this box of wine is really delicious. People hear 'box of wine' and they think, 'Oh jeez. Oh no, I would never drink that, because it probably tastes like a box. But, you guys, it doesn't taste like a box at all. It just tastes like wine. I wonder how good this microphone thingy is. Can you hear me pouring more wine? Well, I'm not actually pouring it. I've got my box of Franzia Sunset Blush sitting right next to me on my kitchen table and it's got a plastic spout where I just push the button. *Glug-glug-glug*—I'm inserting sound effects just in case you can't hear it. Aaand… instant glass of wine!" I take a big gulp from the glass I've already refilled twice before and continue to ramble.

"Okay, so… okay, podcast. Podcast. It's my podcast! Heidi's… Heidi's Podcast. Whatever. Okay, so… uhhh, what am I going to talk about? Like, who would listen to this? Who cares? Who would even listen…." I stop to take another swig of cheap wine and start over.

"Hi! This is the podcast of a woman who used to be a kindergarten teacher and got fired because of budget cuts, and now she got hired at a place where she sits around listening to people read dirty books all day. It's like… worse than that time I played Cards Against Humanity at my cousin's New Year's Eve party after our parents had gone home, and the card said, *'During sex, I like to think about…'* and the only card I had left in my hand was one that said *'Butt Stuff'* and I was so confused, because who thinks about going to the bathroom during sex? But then my cousin's girlfriend explained it to me and I wanted to die and I kept shouting, 'People really do that? But why?'"

I snort, swirling the liquid inside my glass. "Oh my God… I thought I blocked that out." And I begin yet again. "Okay, so… hi! This is a podcast about…. What is it even about? You know what? This podcast is about the fact that I am so stuck right now. I can't do what my mom wants me to do. I don't have a job my parents will ever brag to their friends about. I obviously can't do what Laura's doing next door with my neighbor, because I don't know how to say all those dirty things and bat my eyelashes and be so… Laura. I know how to fall into bushes though, let me tell you. I'm really good at that. I'm a bush ninja. Does anyone need to hire a bush ninja? I'm available evenings and weekends after dark. Hey, it's Heidi's Bush Ninja Show, where she tries to avoid falling into rosebushes, because bleeding isn't sexy."

I chug the rest of my wine, definitely feeling sorry for myself, and then point at the microphone as if it's a person I'm trying to convince. "I'm also well-skilled in drooling so hard over my shirtless neighbor that I drop a box of podcast equipment all over my walkway, and he has to come over in all his shirtless, bare-chested glory and smile at me so... shirtlessly. What the heck?"

I let out a belch before asking, "So, I don't know. What else is in this box?" I hold the offending object in the air. "Oh no. I'm not gonna read that. Definitely not gonna read that. Did I mention my neighbor was shirtless when he read the back cover of this thing? Oh, you probably can't see what I'm holding, can you? That's probably for the best. I don't want anyone to know this book is even in my house, let alone that I touched it. But you should have heard him reading the blurb, with all that stuff he has going on up top and his no-shirt-wearing, muscly man muscles, and all that sweaty shirtlessness, and those dimples.... Is it hot in here all of a sudden? I feel warm. Maybe I should have more wine so I forget about how hot I am."

Even though I'm wasted and will definitely regret it in the morning, I refill my glass once more while chanting, "Glug-glug-glug, I'm spouting more wine into my glass. Do-do-do! I'm just gonna set this book waaay over here on the other side of the table and pretend it's not even sitting there, silently judging me. I should read something though. I gotta read something. I'll just read something, because then I don't even have to think about what I'm gonna say! Oh, this will be fun! Hold on, I'll be right back. I'm gonna get a book from my shelf on the other side of the room."

I hop out of my chair excitedly before the world spins beneath my feet, and I walk with my arms spread for balance, feeling like I'm on a ship as I make my way to my bookcase.

"I'm back! I grabbed one of my favorites. I'll read this Lisa Puffinbarger book about the guy in the buggy going down the road to the covered bridge. There was a good covered bridge scene; let me find it. Okay, chapter three. *Hyrum Yoder had always been in love with his neighbor on the next farm over, Sarah Bender. The pale pink bonnet that adorned her head matched the color of her lips that—*' Uuugh, I can't do this! I swear, this is a sweet, beautiful scene about Sarah finally realizing Hyrum is in love with her, and it's all because of the covered bridge and because she realizes there's so much more to him than just a man who churns butter for his family. But after what I heard at work today, everything Hyrum says about Sarah suddenly seems so dirty, and I can't read this without emphasizing the word *'churn'* because all I can hear in my head is producer Dave telling a narrator he thinks it needs to be hotter, and there shouldn't be anything hot or dirty about butter churning!" I huff, blowing a piece of hair that's fallen into my face.

I put my elbows on the table then drop my forehead into my hands, closing my eyes. "I can't do this. Why am I so boring? This is so sad. I'm just gonna get another glass of wine. Yay, Heidi's Wine Show! But it's more like, whine show. Waaah, why is my life so boring?"

I murmur to myself more than the recording device in front of me, "Okay, Heidi. Pretend you are not a loser."

I sit up straight, ready to give it one more go, but then I promptly deflate. "Oh my God. This is a mess. I'm a mess. I'm a boring former kindergarten teacher who can't even talk about an Amish romance without blushing. How do I expect my hot, muscly neighbor— with dimples that make me feel like melted butter—to even give me a second glance? I can't. Because I'm pathetic. And now I want butter. I want a big old buttery sculpture of Princess Kay of the Milky Way sitting on my table now. I would eat her face right off," I sniff, standing to look over the equipment.

"Did this even work? This thing probably didn't even record. I'm gonna get more Franzia and see if it worked. Or maybe I'll just Netflix something."

Chapter 6

"I COULD HAVE died last night and you don't even care."

My mother's overly dramatic voice in my ear feels like someone is driving nails right through my skull. Pressing my palm against my forehead, I close my eyes and lean back in the computer chair behind the reception desk at EdenMedia. Thankfully, it's been a quiet morning so far. A few narrators were already hard at work when I got here an hour ago, and I made sure they had everything they needed before running away from the sound booths and back to the safety of the reception area before they started recording.

I know better than to drink on a work night. The empty box of wine on my kitchen table this morning, along with the podcast equipment strewn all around it, tells me I made more than one poor choice last night, but all I can remember is sitting at the table talking to myself. And watching a really unhealthy number of episodes of *Fuller House*.

"Mom, if you would have died last night, I'm pretty

sure you wouldn't have called me twelve times and sent eight text messages."

"Your father could have been using my phone to tell you I died. I went through eighteen hours of labor with you, without the comfort of pain medication, and you don't even care that I might be lying here right now, dead. I would have died without my daughter even telling me about her job interview."

I silently mouth the whole "eighteen hours of labor" spiel right along with her, since that's always her go-to way of making me feel guilty.

"I've already gotten three phone calls this morning asking how your interview went, and I had to pretend like I have a thoughtful, loving daughter who cares about her own mother and tells her about what's going on with her life," she continues.

"I'm sorry, Mom. It was a long day, and I was exhausted when I got home. Didn't you get my text that I got the job and everything was fine?"

Yes, I took the chicken's way out and sent her a text instead of calling her back. I was in no way prepared last night to explain to her what they do here at EdenMedia. The fact that I picked up her call a few minutes ago without giving it a second thought is just a reminder that I'm not running on all cylinders this morning, because I'm *still* not prepared. I doubt I'll ever be.

Sheesh, how much did I drink last night, and what did I do with that equipment?

"How was I supposed to know that text was even from you? You could have been abducted on your way home and that was your kidnapper sending a text just to throw me off. That happened to Karen Mendleson. You remember Karen Mendleson's daughter from high school. Alicia Mendleson. You two always had lockers next to each other, because it was alphabetical order. Pretty girl, except for when she smiled, because she had that problem with her front teeth, but just the sweetest thing and always so polite. She works for Dr. Stanford's office as a medical assistant, and since they have a good dental plan, she finally got her teeth fixed with braces. She was on her way home from work a few months ago and stopped to get gas. Not at Colony Plaza, because their gas is always ten cents higher than everywhere else. She went to Kwik Trip, but since there was a water main break on East Main Street, she had to take Yellowstone Trail to Vista Boulevard. So, she gets her gas and heads to Karen's house for dinner. Karen was making lasagna, and she doesn't use those precooked noodles like I told her to, so of course it took over an hour for the lasagna to cook, and Alicia *still* wasn't there, even though she'd sent her mother a text telling her she would be there in a few minutes. Poor Karen. She still talks about that night."

My headache grows increasingly worse with each word my mother speaks.

"Mom, Alicia got a flat tire. She didn't get kidnapped," I remind her, having spoken to Alicia at church the day after this happened where we both commiserated about how crazy our mothers are.

"But Karen didn't know that! Just wait until you have your own children, Heidi, and you'll understand the pain I go through on a daily basis worrying about you. Now, tell me all about this job. I've got a pan of toffee bars in the oven and have thirty minutes until they're finished."

A chime echoes through the reception area, indicating someone just walked through the front doors. I quickly sit up straight in my chair, thankful I'm literally being saved by the bell. Holding the phone between my cheek and shoulder, I quickly move the mouse around on top of the desk to bring the computer back to life to check the calendar and see who's scheduled to be here.

"It's just a typical office job where I answer phones and send emails. It's fine, I'm fine, and there's not much else to tell right now."

At least nothing I want to tell her over the phone. Or ever.

I do a double take when I see the name listed on the calendar, wondering if I'm still a little wine drunk from last night. There's no way that's correct. No way at all. When I sense someone standing in front of my desk, I slowly look up from the computer screen, and my mouth drops open.

"I went through eighteen hours of—"

Pulling the phone away from my ear, I quickly end the call, cutting my mother off midsentence, knowing

I'm going to pay for that later. And by "later" I mean right this second, since my phone immediately starts buzzing in my hand. I don't have to look down at it to know it's her calling back. I quickly press the button on the side of the phone to silence it, open the top drawer of the desk, and toss it inside, never taking my eyes off the man standing in front of me.

"Sorry, didn't want to interrupt," he says with a kind smile. "I'm Jameson Kenter. I think I'm on the schedule to do some recording this morning."

I blink my eyes a few times, wondering if I'm dreaming. When the tall, devastatingly handsome man I'd recognize anywhere is still standing on the other side of my desk, I know I'm awake and this definitely isn't a dream.

"You're Jameson Kenter," I whisper in awe.

With his short, jet-black hair and striking green eyes, Jameson Kenter would make any woman act like a fool in his presence, even if he wasn't one of Hollywood's hottest up-and-coming actors. Even though action movies aren't really my thing, I've seen everything he's done, because he's just so pretty to look at, on top of being a great actor who does all of his own stunt work.

Jameson chuckles softly and nods, reaching his arm across the desk with his hand out.

I look at his hand, back up to his face, then down at his hand again before I realize what he's doing and quickly leap up to shake it. The back of my knees smack into the seat of the chair and it goes flying backward, crashing into the wall behind me. I'm so busy wincing at the loud noise it makes that at least it stops me from giggling like a fool when Jameson's large, warm hand wraps around mine and he gives it a firm shake.

My cell phone starts buzzing loudly again from inside the desk drawer, bouncing all around the metal interior, making an even bigger racket than my chair flying into the wall. Dropping Jameson's hand, I quickly reach out and slam the drawer closed to quiet the noise, giving him an apologetic smile when he chuckles again.

"I'm sorry. It's only my second day here, and I have to say I'm a little surprised to see a real, live movie star standing in front of me. No one told me there'd be famous people walking through the doors. You're like, *really* famous. And tall. I didn't think you'd be so tall. Are you filming a movie that takes place in a recording studio or something?" I ramble.

Jameson smiles at me and casually slides his hands into the front pockets of his jeans. There's just something about his kind eyes and how *normal* he seems that makes me feel at ease.

"I actually just finished filming in Minneapolis. I was hired to narrate a book, and my agent was able to find this place and squeeze me in while I'm in town," he explains. "I haven't had a vacation in a while, so I thought I'd take some time off after recording just to lay low and check out the sights."

"*You're* narrating a book? At EdenMedia?" I asked in astonishment. Pressing my palms flat against the top of the desk, I lean across it and lower my voice. "You know what kind of books they narrate here, right?"

Jameson's smile deepens, and even though it doesn't have the same effect on me that Brent's smile does, it's a nice smile, and I really can't believe I'm standing here having a conversation with *the* Jameson Kenter like it's no big deal and it happens every day.

Working here might actually have some perks.

"I hope it's romance novels, since that's what I was hired to narrate. Otherwise, I'm in the wrong place." He quirks his lips in a smile.

"Oh, and you're definitely in the right place if you're here to narrate romance novels, if that's what you call them. At least you won't be narrating a Penelope Sharp book, since someone's already doing that. I think my ears are still on fire after listening to a few lines from *that* thing yesterday, let me tell you."

"*Sleeping with my Secretary* or *Falling for my Secretary*?"

"I…. You…. Oh my. You've heard of those books?"

"I should hope so. Penelope Sharp's my wife."

Forget the loud, annoying buzzing still coming from my desk drawer. That sound you hear right now is my head exploding from embarrassment.

"You can stop apologizing." Jameson laughs as I guide him down the hallway to the empty recording booth he'll be spending the rest of the day in.

"I really am sorry. I had no idea, and I never would have said something like that otherwise." I push open the door to the booth to allow him to enter ahead of me.

"I told you, it's fine. She doesn't really publicize that Penelope Sharp is Aubrey Kenter's pen name, because she doesn't want people to think she's using my fame to sell books. There's no way you could have known," he explains as I hover in the doorway and watch him get comfortable on the stool in front of the microphone.

Everyone who's ever heard of Jameson Kenter knows about his marriage to Aubrey. It was the fairytale of the century as the world watched the two of them fall in love all over social media. She was just a small-town, regular, everyday woman from Ohio who decided to do something crazy a few years ago and got a job as an extra in one of his movies when they were filming in Cleveland. Jameson and Aubrey met over Danishes at the craft services table, and now they live happily ever after in Hollywood.

"Heidi, I'm gonna need your help testing out the microphone levels," Dave states in a rush as he walks into the room behind me and sits down at the DAW, giving Jameson a wave from the other side of the glass like it's perfectly normal there's a famous Hollywood actor sitting a few feet away.

Obviously, this kind of thing happens all the time and he's not even fazed by it. I'm so busy wondering what other famous person might make an appearance at some point that I completely miss what he just said.

"I'm sorry. What did you say?"

Dave fiddles with a few of the buttons on the board without looking up at me.

"Bethany is late, as usual. That woman is a pain in my ass, but don't tell her I said that, since she's one of the most popular female narrators out there right now. She's supposed to be narrating the chapters from the woman's point of view in this book, and before I can get Jameson started, I need to set the sound levels. Just go on in there and read a few lines of whatever you want from the iPad," Dave says with a wave of his hand.

Not wanting to cause any more problems than I already have this morning by putting my foot in my mouth with Jameson, I move the rest of the way into the recording booth and try not to throw up when Jameson hands me an extra pair of headphones with a smile.

A flash of a memory from last night hits me, and I start to recall something about reading one of my books out loud for some reason, but I quickly push it out of my mind as I take the headphones from Jameson.

Sliding them on my head and over my ears as I get closer to him, I glance at the iPad lying on the stand in front of us. It's already pulled up to the first chapter and I calm down a little, closing my eyes and taking a few deep breaths. There's no way the very first chapter will start with anything even remotely crazy or dirty. I would assume there should be some sort of build-up to an... *intimate moment*, right? Like a nice dinner or a dancing scene. This shouldn't be too bad.

"Whenever you're ready, Heidi."

Dave's voice echoes through my headphones, and I take another calming breath before opening my eyes, and giving Jameson a nervous smile.

"You'll do fine. Just pretend you're by yourself and no one else is listening. That's what I usually do. It makes things a little easier," Jameson advises.

I give him a nod, turn my head to look at the iPad, and just go for it.

"He looks down at me with fire in his eyes, and before I can even take my next breath, his body slams against mine, filling... filling...' Uh, filling my glass with some nice, cold, refreshing water. Oh, this water is so cold and delicious. I'll just drink it and go home," I adlib, refusing to read the rest of that sentence when, contrary to what Jameson said, I absolutely cannot pretend like no one else is listening.

Where's the dinner? Where's the dancing? Where's the freaking romance? They're just gonna get right down to it in chapter one?

I hear Dave laugh through my headphones, but I continue staring down at the iPad, refusing to glance over at Jameson, knowing he's looking over my shoulder at the words I couldn't bring myself to say.

Who knew there were so many words to describe female body parts? And why do they have to be so... wet? That sounds like a medical condition the poor character should get checked out.

"Well, that was... interesting. I got what I needed though," Dave says.

I quickly remove the headphones and set them down on the stand next to the iPad.

"That was awful. I can't believe I did that," I mutter.

"It wasn't that bad. It was very... enthusiastic," Jameson states, biting down on his bottom lip to keep himself from laughing.

"I don't know how you do this. Reading books like this out loud. Or how your wife writes them, for that matter. I'm sorry. That was me being rude. Again. I should ask your wife for some tips." I laugh. "At least you're famous and people would pay good money to listen to whatever book you'd read. I don't even think people would pay twenty-five cents to listen to me. Heidi's Discount Erotica, you get whatcha pay for!"

Before Jameson can reply, Dave sticks his head into the recording booth.

"Seriously, that wasn't a complete disaster, aside from you not actually reading what was written," Dave teases. "It was much better than that podcast of yours I stumbled upon this morning when I googled you just for the hell of it and found your blog. You need more practice with that, although the whole butter thing was hilarious. Don't read anymore of those Amish books.

You'll never get your shirtless neighbor to fall in love with you reading those things. Take home some of the extra books that are lying around the break room and practice reading those. Next time I need you to test mic levels, maybe you won't turn that alarming shade of red."

With that, Dave pulls his head out of the room and goes back to sit behind his desk as memories of what I may or may not have done with all that podcast equipment last night come crashing back into my hungover brain.

No, no, no. Please tell me I did not drunk record a podcast and actually put it on the internet!

"So, tell me about this podcast Dave speaks of. Particularly the part about the shirtless neighbor," Jameson says with a wag of his eyebrows.

Forget about my ears still being on fire after listening to Steve record that book yesterday, or Brent knowing I had a dirty book in my possession, or embarrassing myself by poking fun at Jameson's wife's books. My face is so hot right now you could cook an egg on it.

"Dave doesn't know what he's talking about. I'm pretty sure he drinks at work. Heavily. He might need a twelve-step program."

Oh jeez. I'm gonna get fired. I don't even want this job, but I definitely don't want to get fired. Again.

"If you tell me, then when my wife comes to visit tomorrow, I'll have her explain to you how she got over her fears of writing sex scenes. You kind of remind me of Aubrey when I first met her. She's crazy adorable and was so shy when we first met she practically whispered everything she said to me. Now, she throws out words like *pulsing cock* in the middle of dinner." He laughs. "She's also dubbed herself the queen of matchmaking. I'm sure she'd jump at the chance to help you out with your neighbor."

Well, here we go. I wanted something new and exciting in my life. I don't think it gets much more thrilling than listening to Jameson Kenter casually talking about a pulsing... *thing* and offering his wife up to me for help.

Hmm, Heidi's Discount Erotica. That actually has a nice ring to it.

Chapter 7

I STARE DOWN at my phone and sigh heavily as I walk out of my garage and head toward the back of my house. All of the homes on this street, as well as all the others in the neighborhood, have their garages separate from the houses. There is an alley directly behind our houses that is just lined with everyone's garages. Even though this is a small town and the crime rate is pretty low, it can still be a little creepy, which is why I only park back here when it's still light outside.

Not even the excitement of meeting Jameson today and chitchatting with him like we've been friends for years or the nervousness of wondering if a serial killer is lying in wait for me in the alley can put extra pep in my step. I drag my feet along the sidewalk, my shoulders hunched in shame. I should have just pretended like that stupid drunk podcast I recorded the other night never happened, but as soon as the memory of what I did came back when Dave so kindly pointed it out in front of Jameson, I got curious. And I checked my blog to see if there were any comments, hoping against hope that

Dave was the only human being on the planet who heard that thing.

I don't even know why I still have a blog. It was just the thing you did in college, so I followed the herd and randomly posted silly stories about stuff that happened at school or recipes I found online that I thought sounded good.

I pause in the middle of the walkway between my house and Brent's, rereading the two comments that were left on my blog post with the podcast on it.

That was hilarious! You need more smut in your life. Go get 'em, tiger!

You suck. Never record a podcast ever again. Go eat farts, Heidi.

You can probably guess which one was Dave's comment. The second one was left by "Anonymous." I took a chance and put myself out there for anyone and their brother to hear, and this person gets to escape behind the anonymity of a computer to insult me. Sure, I didn't exactly *plan* on recording a podcast and uploading it to my blog, and I had no clue what I was doing, but still. They could at least have the decency to use their real name if they're going to tell me to eat farts. Luckily, when I checked my blog stats before leaving EdenMedia, it said only three people listened to the podcast. I can handle that, I guess. Three people isn't bad. Two people commented, and the third person was probably so horrified they couldn't even bring themselves to say anything, good or bad. I mean, if you don't have anything nice to say, you shouldn't say it at all, so I like that third person the best right now.

"Fancy meeting you here."

A squeak of surprise flies out of my mouth and I quickly look up from my phone to find Brent standing right next to me on my walkway.

I quickly press my phone against my chest to hide the screen. At least none of those three people who listened to my podcast were Brent.

At least, I *hope* none of those people were Brent. Oh, God. Oh no! What if he was the third person? I mean, the odds are against it. But what if for some strange reason he decided to Google me, just like Dave did? I still haven't listened to that stupid thing again, but going by the comments Dave made at work, I definitely said way too much about Brent. Okay, worst-case scenario— the third person was Brent. But maybe I never said his name and he has no idea I was talking about him. Maybe I just referred to him as my "shirtless neighbor." Really, I could have been referring to anyone on this street. Mr. Charmichael two houses down likes to take his shirt off in the summer and relax on his front porch after a long day of working at the local manufacturing plant. Yes, Mr. Charmichael is also a sixty-three-year-old man who's covered in so much dark body hair that I often wonder if Mrs. Charmichael has to brush it every night so it doesn't tangle.

But still. I could be attracted to Mr. Charmichael. Brent has no idea what my taste in men is.

Ugh. Maybe I should just find a new place to live.

"I saw you pulling into your garage the same time as me and thought I'd come over and see how work was today," Brent says. "Better than your first day?"

I'm more than a little surprised he actually took the time to walk all the way over here to my walkway just to talk to me. Not unpleasantly so.

Since Brent works for a local construction company, we typically keep the same hours, so it's not unusual for us to get home at the same time during the week, but he normally doesn't stop to chitchat.

I realize I'm still standing here staring at him in shock and quickly look down at my phone. My inability to stop gawking at his dimples or sighing whenever I hear his voice would be a dead giveaway of what kind of man I'm attracted to.

Why couldn't Brent be a mean, average-looking man? It would be much easier to talk to him if he wasn't so good-looking and nice and didn't make me feel all tingly whenever he looked at me.

At least he's wearing a shirt this time.

"Yeah, well, contrary to what X-rated movies say, it's kind of frowned upon for a construction worker to use dangerous power tools without wearing a shirt."

My head whips up from my phone to find Brent

smiling at me with humor sparkling in his eyes, and I realize I said that last thought in my head out loud.

"Oh, I was just concerned about your skin! You know, all that sun shining down on you all day... skin cancer is no joke. If you ever need to borrow some sunscreen, I have plenty!"

Excellent, Heidi. There's nothing more attractive than talking about cancer.

Brent takes a step closer to me, and all of a sudden, I'm surrounded by the smell of him. There's a faint hint of woodsy cologne, but it's mainly just soap and *man*. I really want to avoid any and all eye contact with him, since it seems to constantly turn me into a bumbling idiot, but it's impossible to look away when he's standing right in my personal space and I can feel the heat from his body. I've never noticed his blue eyes have specks of gold surrounding the pupil, and they're so gorgeous I don't think I'd be able to stop staring at them even if someone physically pulled me away from him.

"You never answered my question. How was work today?"

His voice is like a warm, gentle breeze floating all around me, and I feel like I've been put under a spell. I can't move, I can't breathe, and I can't think. All I can do is stand perfectly still, wondering what Brent would do if I could be bold and fearless and tell him I don't give a crap about work; I just want to continue watching his lips move and wonder if they taste like the peppermint I can smell on his breath, since he's standing so close.

"W-w-work was great," I stutter softly. "I actually met someone famous today. Jameson Kenter. Have you seen his movies? He's much taller in person. And even better looking. And so nice. He's going to be there every day for a while recording a book."

"Wow. Jameson Kenter, huh? Sounds like a great way to spend your day at work, with someone so good-looking and nice." Brent smiles.

He's smiling at me, but there's something off about his smile. It doesn't quite reach his eyes. I've spent a lot of time studying Brent's eyes, and whenever he's amused or happy about something, little crinkles form around the corners. I don't see crinkles. There are no crinkles. *Where are the crinkles?*

"But you're more better and good-lookinger!" I quickly reassure him.

Oh my God, I was a teacher! That sentence is a travesty to the entire English language!

"I mean, you are a super nice guy. And you're better looking. I'll just stop talking now."

My stomach does a weird little flip-flop when I see the crinkles I've been waiting for form around Brent's eyes as he smiles at me.

"You think I'm nice and good-looking?" he asks, and I swear I see a twinkle in his eyes.

"You should just forget I said that. It's not like you

need the reassurance. I'm sure you've looked in a mirror. Unless you're a vampire." I snort, forming my fingers into a cross and holding it up in front of his face. "Nope. You didn't instantly burst into flames."

I snort again then immediately wish I could snap my fingers and transport myself elsewhere. Like Siberia. I'm being so *Heidi* right now I'm getting on my own nerves.

I'm embarrassed and mortified and I'm covering it up with lame humor. I can't believe I thought Brent might have been jealous there for a second when I mentioned Jameson. It just proves what a mess I am. Why would Brent care who I spend my work days with? He wouldn't. At all. Brent is hot. Heidi is not. Heidi is always told she's *cute* and *adorable*. Heidi does not attract a man the likes of Brent. Heidi attracts men who were forced to go out with her when two meddling mothers got together over coffee.

Heidi really needs to stop thinking about herself in third person.

"Well, I don't want to keep you. I'm sure you have much more important things to do than stand here listening to me embarrass myself," I tell Brent with a nervous laugh as I start backing away from him.

I too have a lot of important things to do. Like research flights to Siberia.

The adorable, lopsided grin I love so much is in full force on Brent's face as he stands there on the walkway, watching me hustle backward away from him as fast as I can without falling and making an even bigger fool of myself.

"Well, when you have some free time after hanging with famous people, don't forget you promised to teach me all about living in Minnesota."

Holy cow, I can't believe he remembered that. It was something nice and neighborly I threw out the day we met, when he caught me watching him unload boxes from the moving van.

Which is just another thing to add to my list of why I'm so ridiculous. If I had any guts at all, I would have made a list of all the things I love about Minnesota, including all the places we could visit and I could introduce him to, and then let him pick where he wanted to go first. But I have no guts. Instead, I have the ability to call someone *more better* and accuse them of being a vampire.

"Okay, you betcha!" I shout over-excitedly as I turn away from him and walk faster toward my house.

"And Heidi!" Brent shouts after me, my feet never faltering in their quick escape from him. "I think you're good lookinger too!"

I practically run the rest of the way up the walk to my house, refusing to let myself think about the fact that Brent is still standing where I left him, watching me the entire time, or what he just shouted to me. I'm sure he just said that to be funny, because I sounded like an idiot when I said it to him. There's no way he thinks I'm good lookinger.

It really is a blessing I'm no longer molding young minds.

As soon as I get into the safety of my house and close the door, I slump my back against it and let out a weary sigh.

"Why can't I just be cool and light and flirty without looking and sounding like an idiot?" I mumble to myself, glancing over at my laptop and the podcast equipment still lying all over my kitchen table.

I don't want to suck anymore.

As soon as that thought pops into my head, I giggle to myself, thinking about my podcast and Brent and the stack of books I'd snuck in my purse from the break-room at Eden Media when no one was looking. I think about how Dave and Jameson told me I had a great voice after the sound check earlier. Their exact words were "enthusiastic" and "not a complete disaster." And you know what? I'll take it. At the end of the day, Jameson even tried to make me feel better by saying I was "spirited."

I need to stop thinking that being called spirited and enthusiastic are insults. I like who I am for the most part. I don't want to change into a completely different person. I just need to find a way to be spirited, enthusiastic, *and* courageous.

With a determined lift of my chin, I march over to my kitchen table, upend my purse, and watch all the books fall to the table in a shower of half-naked men and suggestive titles.

Once I start something, I refuse to quit. I started a podcast, and even though it was a mess, I'm not going to quit until I get it right.

Heidi's Discount Erotica, here I come.

Chapter 8

Heidi's Discount Erotica, Episode 2

"*H*EY, ALL YOU... three people who tuned in last time! Welcome to Heidi's Discount Erotica Podcast, do-do-do!

"I don't know why I sang that little jingle. I have a vague recollection of doing that in my first podcast, so I'm just gonna go with it. Heidi's Discount Erotica now has a jingle, yay!

"First of all, I'd like to apologize for my initial podcast. I'm pretty sure you've guessed I don't exactly have experience in this sort of thing. Shout-out to Anonymous for telling me I suck. I did. I do. I can be woman enough to accept that. But please refrain from telling me to eat farts, because that's just hurtful. Now, I know I need to make some changes so I can finally figure out what makes me happy in life. The first change I'll be making is doing whatever I can to prove Anonymous

73

wrong. I'm not gonna suck anymore! This podcast is going to be the non-suckiest podcast out of all of them!

"Heh, heh, heh, sorry! I said… suck a lot, didn't I? It would be funnier if you could see all of the books I've got spread out on my kitchen table right next to me. I should take a poll. How many times do you think that word is said in one of these books, not referring to a sweet, delicious lollipop? I'm just gonna flip through one of these and stop on a random page to… oh… oh my. That's…. There's… there's a…. You guys! Oh jeez. There's a lollipop scene. I can't… huh. That's very… inventive. I didn't know you could put that… there… and then…. Holy jeez.

"Okay, we'll just put that one aside for now. I was going to give my second apology in regards to my heavy consumption of boxed wine in the last podcast, but what's the point? It's quite clear I'm going to need to be a little tipsy to get over this initial hump. I can't very well continue standing in my yard silently screaming for my neighbor to kiss me and being too afraid to do anything about it. And just so you know, when I say 'neighbor,' I could be talking about anyone. It doesn't *have* to be the one who lives right next to me. It could very well be someone across the street. Or two blocks down. It could be anyone, really. Just because the one who lives right next to me has the most beautiful eyes I've ever seen, a voice that makes me feel all warm and gooey, and smells like sunshine and soapy man doesn't mean I'm talking about him.

"Now that we've gotten that cleared up, I don't really have much else to say in this episode. If you decided to tune in again after the last one, thank you. I promise this will get better.

"Tomorrow at work, I get to hang out with famous people. I can't tell you who they are right now, but I can tell you that I might be getting some much-needed advice from them. And since they're both kind of experts at the whole 'doing something scary because you know it will be good for you' thing, I have a great feeling about this. I'm actually excited to go into work tomorrow! And to tell you guys all about it!

"In the meantime, if you have any advice for me, I'll take it! Have you ever tried to break out of the mold you've been in since you were born? Have you spent your entire life making everyone around you happy, and you realized in all that time, you forgot about making yourself happy? This is my conundrum, folks. This is why I hope you'll stick with me. I don't know what I'm doing, and this journey will probably involve a lot of wine and stumbles along the way, but it's happening. I'm taking the leap. I'm doing something scary and crazy, because even though it's scary and crazy, it's also pretty darn exciting. I'm doing what I want for a change and not worrying about anyone else.

"But, um, if you happen to know my mother, please, don't tell her about this. It will be our little secret. And it's not because I'm already going back on my word and worrying about someone else. Seriously, I fear for my own life if my mother catches wind of this. And I'm just starting to live my life. I don't want to die before I get to explore... you know... the many uses of... lollipops... with my neighbor. Who could be anyone that lives anywhere on this street.

"I know, I know! I'm giggling. I can't help it. I'll work on that. Lollipops... who knew?

"Heidi's podcast, episode two, over and out."

Chapter 9

"**W**ELL, IF IT isn't my favorite niece."

My feet stutter to a stop right in front of the door to EdenMedia and my head whips up in surprise.

"Aunt Margie, what are you doing here?"

I nervously glance behind her, and she laughs at me.

"Don't worry; your mom's not with me. Your deep, dark secret of working for a company who peddles porn is safe with me."

"What? How did you...? I don't...."

Aunt Margie shakes her head at me, grabbing the book out of my hand I forgot I had cradled to my chest as I walked into work. I try not to fidget uncomfortably as she flips through the pages.

"Unlike your mother, I know how to Google. I did some research on EdenMedia after she told me about your new job," she tells me, stopping on a page in the middle and scanning the words. "Oh, hey! Look what they're doing with a lollipop. Who knew?"

Snatching the book back out of her hands, I shove it into my purse where I should have put it when I left my house this morning. I blame my lack of discretion on the small amount of sleep I got last night. All because of that stupid book. Or maybe I should say, that absolutely amazing, wonderful, intense book that I couldn't put down until I'd read the last word.

"What are you doing here? I mean, I'm happy to see you and all, but Mom still doesn't exactly know what goes on here. I'm going to tell her; I just need some time," I quickly explain.

"*Some* time? Kiddo, you're going to need at least thirty years for your mom's head to stop exploding once she finds out." Aunt Margie chuckles. "I'm proud of you, if it's any consolation. You deserve a little excitement in your life. Don't worry; I won't say a word."

My mom and my aunt are as close as sisters can be, considering they are polar opposites. And even though I don't have a sister, I do understand the bond they share and how, under normal circumstances, my Aunt Margie's loyalty would always go to my mom first. If my life was in jeopardy or I was doing something illegal, I know my aunt wouldn't hesitate to tell my mom everything. But since I'd never get myself into a situation like that, it's nice to have someone on my side who will keep my secrets. Like that time the summer after my senior year of high school, right before I left for college, when I told my mom I was spending the night at my aunt's house, and instead, I spent the night with my boyfriend and lost my virginity. That's a secret I know Aunt Margie will take to her grave. Not just because of the personal and private nature of the situation, but because if my mom knew Margie lied for me to do something like *that*, we'd both be dead.

"I'm definitely getting plenty of excitement working here," I tell her. "These books…. I had no idea. I thought they were just about the dirty stuff with no storyline and no plot, but they aren't. They're so much more. The women in these books, they take charge of their own lives and learn how to ask for what they want. It's so empowering."

After I finished reading the book at four this morning, I lay there in bed, staring up at the ceiling for another hour, feeling like the biggest fool. I made fun of books like this. I scoffed at the covers and rolled my eyes at the summaries. I've been embarrassed about telling people what kind of books they record at EdenMedia, because I know they'll make the same snap judgements. Now, I just want to tell everyone I know to read these stories and see for themselves that you shouldn't judge a book by its cover. For the first time since I accepted this job, I'm proud of where I work and the kind of books they record here, and I want everyone to know it.

Everyone except my mother, that is.

"Heidi! You get prettier every time I see you!"

My excitement and courage vanishes like a puff of smoke when Sharleen Donaldson walks up next to my aunt with a huge smile on her face, even though one side is puffy and slightly droopy.

"Did I forget to mention I'm here because I drove Sharleen to the dentist next door to get a root canal?" Aunt Margie muses.

I've known Sharleen since birth. She's one of my mom and aunt's closest friends, and out all of the people I could possibly run into outside of work, of *course* it had to be her. I'd almost prefer my mom at this point. Sharleen is a wonderful woman, but she's also the biggest source of gossip in Waconia. When you go to Sharleen's house in the summer, nine times out of ten, she'll be out in her backyard, chatting to a group of neighbors over the fence. If it's in the dead of winter, her home phone is permanently attached to her ear.

If you want to know who stole Roberta Markum's famous apple pie recipe and won first place with it at the county fair, ask Sharleen.

If you think your husband is having an affair, Sharleen can tell you the exact date, time, and location of each time he's been seen in public with someone who isn't you, along with what the other woman was wearing, her date of birth, and the last three jobs she held.

If you want to know why there was a sheriff's car parked along the curb of someone's home last Friday night, Sharleen will know which deputy it was, how long he stayed in the house, and what kind of cookie bars he had in a Tupperware container when he left.

If a stray cow was found walking along County Road

10, Sharleen can tell you how long it's been walking, if it stopped to eat anything, what farmer it belongs to, which part of the farmer's fence was missing a few boards, and the reason for the great cow escape.

"Is this where you're working now? EdenMedia, huh? Your mom told me you got a new job in Eden Prairie, but she didn't know the name of the company," Sharleen says with a lopsided smile as she looks at the sign hanging on the building behind me. "My face feels funny. Do you hear bells? Margie, is there a bell ringing somewhere?"

My aunt pats Sharleen on the back and leans toward me, lowering her voice.

"Sharleen had a lot of laughing gas and it hasn't worn off yet. I doubt she'll even remember this conversation." Aunt Margie gives me a wink.

Thank heaven for small favors.

"So, Sharleen, did you hear about—"

"EdenMedia, EdenMedia…" Sharleen mutters to herself, cutting me off, still staring at the company sign behind me. "Wait. I've heard of this company. They record books. They record… oh. Oh! Ooohhh!"

I actually see the lightbulb go on in her brain, and no amount of laughing gas will deter the woman at this point. This does not bode well for me.

"Heidi Larson! Does your mother know what they do here?"

She speaks in a loud stage whisper, bringing her hand

up to the side of her face and shielding it, refusing to make eye contact with my place of employment now that she's put two and two together.

I resent that she's treating me like a child, but even more annoyed that everyone in town seems to know about EdenMedia but me.

"I mean, of course Peggy knows what they do here," she continues, her hand still blocking her face from the EdenMedia sign, like it will jump down from above the door and rip off all her clothes if she even glances at it. "It's not like you'd take a brand new job and not tell her all about it. It's a very… interesting job. Margie, how do you feel about your niece working here?"

Sharleen looks over at my aunt, and the two of us share a smile, because we know exactly what's going to happen next. Minnesotans are nice, to a fault. Even if they don't agree with something, they will find the nicest way to state that. If they see a movie, absolutely hated it, and someone asks them what they thought of it, they will use such phrases as *"It was… interesting"* or *"Well, it was… different."* Then, they wait and see what the asker of the question's opinion is to know whether or not they can word-vomit how they really feel or if they need to continue being diplomatic. They do this so they don't put their foot in their mouth by saying something that might not be a popular opinion and come back to bite them later on.

"I think it's wonderful," Aunt Margie states with a

smile. "Heidi's going to have so much fun working here, and that's just what she needs."

"Oh, yes! Working here will definitely be... different for her," Sharleen says with a nod while I cover up a snort-giggle with a loud cough. "The books they record here are... interesting. I mean, I've never read one, of course, but I've heard they're... unique."

"You should take one out for a test drive, Sharleen. I bet Heidi has a few stashed in that purse of hers she could lend you," Aunt Margie suggests with a wink in my direction.

I hug my purse tighter to my body as Sharleen stares at it with her droopy, Novocain-filled mouth partially open in shock.

"She's just kidding!" I reassure Sharleen. "No books here. Nope. None whatsoever. It really is a great job. I'm just working as an administrative assistant at the front desk, so I don't even know about those books she speaks of. I just sit at my desk with my head down and do my work. I don't hear anything that goes on in the recording booths. No clue about anything but answering the phones and replying to emails. It's actually pretty boring. Just your typical office job."

Oh, jeez. I am the absolute worst. What happened to all that pride and excitement I had when I stepped out of my car just a little bit ago?

"Well, that's nice. I'm sure this job will be good for you then. I bet you'll learn a lot of valuable life lessons,"

Sharleen says with a nod.

A car door slams in the parking lot and we all turn when we hear the sound of a man's voice.

I can't stop the smile that lights up my face when I see Jameson holding his cell phone to his ear as he walks in our direction with his head down. If anything will change Sharleen's opinion of where I work and possibly put in a good word with my mom, it will be the fact that she can brag to everyone that she met a real-life movie star and it was all because of me.

"I already recorded that chapter yesterday," Jameson speaks into his phone as he gets closer and closer to us. "Today is the anal sex chapter. I did a quick read-through of it over coffee this morning. I was pleasantly surprised to see the use of lube. And the missionary position. I've read way too many scenes where the butt stuff is done doggy-style and the guy just slams his dick right in there without any warning."

Oh, hey there. Did someone mention valuable life lessons?

Jameson's head lifts up when he steps onto the side-walk a few feet away from us, and he gives me a small wave when he sees me before glancing at the women standing next to me.

Sharleen's eyes are so wide they're on the verge of popping out of her head, and her hand is pressed tightly to her throat, like she's clutching an imaginary set of pearls after what she just heard. Aunt Margie is practical-ly panting like a dog as she blatantly looks him up and down, probably taking mental notes about the things that Jameson said and compiling a list of questions for him on the subject. Me? I'm just standing here cringing.

Jameson quickly ends his call and shoves his phone in his back pocket when he gets next to me, giving Sharleen and Aunt Margie a heart-stopping smile as he gently bumps his shoulder against mine in greeting.

"Heidi, why didn't you tell me you had two gorgeous sisters?" Jameson asks.

Aunt Margie snorts, because she knows he's full of crap, but Sharleen actually titters with glee, her cheeks blushing as she brings her hands up to her head and tries to neaten her hair with her palms.

I make quick introductions, watching in fascination as Sharleen giggles through her handshake with Jameson, and clearing my throat loudly to get my aunt to let go of his hand after clutching it for an uncomfortable length of time.

"Well, we better get inside. Lots of work to do," I say with a smile, grabbing Jameson's elbow and pulling him toward the door of EdenMedia before Aunt Margie thinks it would be a great idea to ask him about the phone conversation we overheard.

Wait! What am I doing? Am I seriously manhandling a Hollywood movie star?

I should let go of his arm. He can walk by himself without me pulling him. And yet, I can't bring myself to let go. Now that I've grabbed onto him, it would be weird to immediately drop his arm like it's on fire, right? And apologize for just reaching out and grabbing him all willy-nilly like he's an unruly child, and not like he's a famous person whom I barely know? Yes, that would be weird *and* awkward.

Oh look! We're already at the door. The voices in my head can stop arguing now.

"It sure was lovely meeting you, Jameson!" Sharleen gushes. "Heidi, I'll be sure to tell your mother what an… interesting job you have."

I sigh in defeat and hang my head. "Have a good day, kiddo!" my aunt shouts to my back as Jameson and I turn around and he opens the door for me. "You should use the *back door* next time. I've heard it's much more thrilling going in the *back way.*"

Jameson chuckles as I quickly walk past him and into the office, shaking my head with a groan.

"I guess it's my turn to apologize. But look on the bright side. Your aunt is hilarious," he says as he follows me over to the front desk and I stow my purse in one of the drawers.

"Oh, it's fine! No big deal!"

Jameson slowly shakes his head at me with a grin.

"You're too nice. My wife would have already threatened to chop off my balls if I said something like that in front of people she knew, without realizing they were standing there."

A tiny smile forms on my lips as an idea begins to

bloom. "How soon before she gets here?" I ask eagerly.

"That's who I was on the phone with. Her plane just landed, so she'll be here as soon as her Uber driver finds the place."

Boldness and self-confidence, here I come! As long as my mom doesn't kill me first.

Chapter 10

"IT WASN'T THAT bad. You were adorably drunk. And look! You had seven more views on the second podcast than you did the first one. It's pretty rare for someone to be absolutely amazing at something the first time they do it. You just need more practice."

Aubrey Kenter, aka Penelope Sharp, aka Jameson's wife, hands my phone back to me in the break room at EdenMedia, where she convinced me to let her listen to my podcasts. I met her exactly an hour ago when she burst through the front doors and flew into Jameson's arms, where I practically swooned in my chair behind the desk, watching them reunite after being apart for several weeks while Jameson was filming. After they broke apart and Jameson introduced us, he disappeared into a recording booth and Aubrey dragged me in here for some girl talk.

Just like with her husband, I immediately felt at ease with her—like I'd known her for years. Since Jameson had already told her a little bit about me and my recent dilemma of being unable to do anything about the crush

I have on Brent, I filled her in on the rest, including how unhappy I've been with my life, and that if we hear a fifty-six-year-old woman screaming from the reception area, *"Heidi Marie Larson, come here right this minute!"* we should run and hide in the nearest closet. Which then led to her convincing me to pull up my podcasts, where I covered my ears and hummed the tune of "Mary Had a Little Lamb" until she was finished.

What surprises me the most about Aubrey is how... *normal* she is. I've seen pictures of her and Jameson on red carpets over the years, and she's always looked so stunning and glamorous. She sits across the small, circular table wearing an oversized Cleveland Indians sweatshirt and a pair of ratty jeans. Her long blonde hair is piled up on top of her head in a messy bun with strands falling out all over the place like she just woke up from a nap, and she's not wearing a stitch of makeup. She's definitely pretty, but I don't feel like I thought I would sitting next to her—small, and inconsequential, and boring, and like an ugly troll who could never catch the eye of her handsome neighbor. I feel like I'm on even footing with her. Like, if we were both out in public somewhere, a man's eyes wouldn't immediately dismiss me and latch onto her.

Aside from the fact that she might get heckled walking down the street for not wearing a Minnesota Twins sweatshirt, she looks like any other Minnesotan. She looks like *me* on a Sunday afternoon when I used to curl up on my couch and grade papers. This is what shocks me the most. That an average, everyday woman—whom I recently found out used to work from home as a medical transcriptionist before she quit to write full time—could get a guy like Jameson Kenter to fall in love with her. It gives me hope.

"I'm finished with my anal sex and it was magical!"

Aubrey and I glance over to the doorway as Jameson walks in.

"That sounded much better in my head," he mutters before walking over to the table and giving Aubrey a kiss on the cheek then taking the seat right next to her. "I've got a thirty-minute break. What are we discussing?"

"I just finished listening to Heidi's podcasts, and we were getting ready to move on to how she's not comfortable around men and what we can do to fix that," Aubrey explains. "Particularly, initiating conversations, flirting, making the first move, stuff like that."

Jameson rests his arm on the back of her chair. I can't stop the sigh that comes out of my mouth when I watch him rest his palm against the back of Aubrey's neck and gently start massaging it.

God, I want that. I want a guy who doesn't even think about doing it, who just sits down next to me and has to touch me.

"I think Heidi is plenty comfortable around men. She's fine with *me*. She's funny and talkative and adorable. And I'm Jameson motherfucking Kenter. It doesn't get much more manly than that."

"If you want to get laid in the next century, never speak those words out loud again."

"Noted. But, another point in Heidi's favor, she made the first move this morning by grabbing my arm and dragging me away from her aunt and friend. She touched a dude without giving it a second thought." Jameson shrugs.

Oh, I gave it a second thought. I gave it so many second thoughts I almost had a nervous breakdown on the sidewalk.

"Um, excuse me," I speak up. "It's true. I do feel comfortable around you, but that's probably because I don't want to make out with you. I mean, no offense. You're really pretty. You're just not my type."

Aubrey throws her head back and laughs, and Jameson presses his hand over his heart.

"You wound me, Heidi. You seriously wound me."

Once Aubrey stops laughing, she leans over to the side away from Jameson and digs around in her purse that's on the floor by her feet. She pops back up a few seconds later with a notebook and pen, smacking them down on the table.

"Okay, let's do a quick little word association thing. It will help clear your mind so I can get a better idea of how you feel about this Brent guy," she explains as she scribbles a few things in her notebook. "I'm going to say some random words. Just say the first thing that pops into your head when you hear them. Don't think about it; just say what comes to you first."

I nod, folding my hands in my lap as she begins.

"Clouds."

"Fluffy," I reply.

"Heart."

"Love," I say with a smile before she really gets down to business and we start the rapid-fire round.

"Tablecloth."

"Dinner."

"Boat."

"Water."

"July."

"Fireworks."

"Tomatoes."

"Garden."

"Brent."

"Sex."

My hand flies up and smacks over my mouth as soon as that word flies out in relation to Brent's name.

Aubrey let's out a loud, whooping cheer, dropping the pen and notebook to throw her hands up in the air.

"Yeah, that's right, you dirty girl! I knew I'd find you in there somewhere!"

"I didn't mean to say that! Wait. *Did* I mean to say that?"

"Of course you meant to say that. You did exactly as I asked. You didn't think; you just said the first word that came to mind. And you, my sweet, adorable, new friend Heidi, have sex on the brain," she says, turning in her chair to look at Jameson. "Honey, don't get me anything for Christmas. This is my present, right here."

Jameson chuckles before giving me a pointed look.

"See? I told you my wife would be over the moon about playing matchmaker. She can't help herself."

"I successfully set up Eric and Lindsey, didn't I?"

"Yes, yes you did. My best friend and your best friend are blissfully happy," Jameson concedes. "But are you forgetting about Alison and Colby?"

"Colby was a manwhore who couldn't keep his dick in his pants, and no one gave me the full disclosure ahead of time about his wandering dick. That doesn't count. Heidi is lovable and charming and beautiful, and she needs someone who will appreciate that. We just need to find out more about this Brent person to see if he fits the bill."

Jameson and Aubrey both look at me expectantly, and I just shrug my shoulders.

"I don't really know that much about him other than he's really nice and sweet and he takes time out of his day to talk to me and ask me how I am."

"And he looks good with his shirt off. Don't forget to add that to the plus column," Aubrey adds.

I can feel a blush heating my cheeks when an image of sweaty, shirtless Brent flashes through my mind.

"That!" Aubrey shouts, making me jump as she points at my face. "That's what we need to work on. Your confidence. We all know you just thought about this guy half naked and sweaty. My husband—who is extremely hot, mind you—is sitting right next to me, and even *I'm* thinking about Brent half naked and sweaty and I've never met the guy. Own it. Be proud of the fact that you think he's hot and want him. There's no shame in that."

"Tell me again how hot you think I am, and I'll forgive you for picturing another man naked," Jameson tells her with a smile.

"Bite me. You already know how hot you are. I am not here to stroke your ego. You have plenty of adoring fans for that."

"I love it when you talk all sweet and romantic to me." He laughs, pushing back his chair and standing up.

My heart flutters as I watch Aubrey reach up, clutch the front of his shirt in her fists, and yank him back down to her.

"How about I make it up to you later by talking dirty to you? I've got a scene I'm working on that needs some research. It involves chocolate sauce, a vibrator, and me wearing nothing but a smile," she speaks softly, her lips right up against his as they stare into each other's eyes.

"Anything in the name of research," Jameson whispers back.

Aubrey gives him a quick kiss before pushing him away. He gives both of us a wave before he walks around the table and out the door to go back to the recording booth.

"Teach me how to do that," I tell her once he's gone.

"How to do what?"

"How to just… grab a guy and pull him close and say stuff like that to him. I want to learn that."

"Ahhh, grasshopper, you've come to the right place," Aubrey replies, rubbing her hands together like an evil mastermind. "We're going to start off small and work our way up. Jameson said you asked him how I could write all those dirty sex scenes knowing people would read them, and that's exactly how I did it. I started small. My first drafts were a mess and read like police reports with just the facts. *Man on bed. Woman lying on top of him. They roll around. Clothes come off. End scene.* I freaked out, thinking about my mom or my grandmother reading it and what they would think of me. It came down to me getting out of my own head and discovering what *I* wanted. It was *my* story and I needed to tell it how *I* wanted to. And I wanted my story to be real. People have sex. People have hot, dirty sex, and it's glorious. You just need to find out how you want to tell your story. How you want to live your own life and do what makes you happy without worrying about what other people will think of you."

"I want to be bold and fearless," I tell her.

"Then, let's make you bold and fearless." She smiles. "Let's do another game. I'm going to say some words, and you just repeat them back to me."

I take a deep breath and nod for her to continue.

"Kiss," she says.

"Kiss," I easily reply.

"Sensual," Aubrey states.

"Sensual," I repeat back.

"His kiss was sensual."

"His kiss was sens-s-s-s-sational. Oh, cripe. What is wrong with me?" I complain. "It's like there's a road-block between my brain and my mouth that won't let me put those words together."

Aubrey laughs, grabbing the seat of her chair and scooting it around the table closer to me.

"I'm giving you two pieces of homework tonight. You're going to do another podcast, and I'm going to give you a few excerpts from the book I'm working on now to practice reading during it."

She quickly reaches over and pats my hand when she sees the look of anxiety on my face.

"Don't worry; they'll be tame. Just something small to start you off so you can work your way up to the good stuff."

"Okay, I can do that. What's my other homework?" I ask.

"You're going to initiate a conversation with Brent."

"Like, *talk* to him? As in, say something to him before he says something to me?"

"Exactly. But I'll start you off small there too. Do you have his cell phone number? You can just send him a text."

"Yes. We exchanged numbers the day he moved in, but I've never used it or anything. I can't just text him! What if he only wanted me to use it in case of an emergency, because he was just being neighborly by giving it to me? Like, if my stove caught on fire, or someone was breaking into my house, or I got a piece of chicken lodged in my throat, or my fridge fell on me?"

"I'm concerned by the idea you'd be in a situation where your refrigerator would fall on you," she muses. "Or that you would take a time-out from choking to death to text someone."

"I am a single woman who lives alone. You have no idea what kind of horrors go through my mind on a daily basis."

Aubrey gives my hand another squeeze of reassurance.

"All you're going to do is text him, tell him you were thinking of him, and ask him how his day was. Easy-peasy."

Easy-peasy my patootie.

"Looks like I'll be stopping by the store on my way home for some more liquid wine." I sigh.

Chapter 11

Heidi's Discount Erotica, Episode 3

"OKAY. WOOOO, WHAT am I doing? Okay. All right. I'm just gonna start. Start by starting. Set down the wine; I've had enough. Maybe one more sip. Okay, *now* I've had enough. I need a cracker. Hold on. I'm gonna hit pause."

*

*

*

"I'm back! Why does wine make me so hungry? It's made from grapes. So, I've basically had like… seventeen pounds of grapes. I shouldn't be hungry. Anyway, welcome to Heidi's Discount Erotica, do-do-do! Tonight, I'm gonna be reading some hot excerpts for you, kind of like the way you might go bungee jumping off Minnehaha Falls—by closing your eyes and just jumping right over the cliff, weeeeeeeee! Or maybe kayaking. Kayaking can be scary, right? I mean, what if your kayak tips over and your legs are stuck in the boat and you can't get out while you're just floating down the river and everyone thinks it's just an empty kayak that got loose, when there's really a person under there trying not to drown and no one can hear you scream, because you're *under water*? Oh, God, I'm having heart palpitations now. Sorry. I need another sip of wine. Okay, that's better.

"Where was I? Oh! Hot excerpts. Yes. So, these were given to me by a friend at work today. I haven't even looked at them yet. She printed them off and then shoved them in my purse. She said it's my homework, along with a text I have to send, but we'll get into that later. I have homework! I feel like one of my students, so this is very exciting. Except the homework my students had was more like coloring a picture of a dog. This is more like one of those adult coloring books with all the swear words in it. You know, without the coloring. So, basically, it's just swear words. But hot swear words.

"Okay. Excerpt… *One.*

"Was that good? Like, kind of breathy? I feel like these should be read all sexy and breathy. Is breathy a word? I'm pretty sure it is. It's a weird word. *B-r-r-r-eathy.*

"Okay, here we go…

" '*In all the years I thought about kissing him again, I pictured it exactly like it was in high school. Clashing teeth, sloppy tongues, and wiping the drool…*' Drool? Eeew. That's gross. I'm sorry. Okay, let's try this again. '...*and wiping the drool away from our chins when it was over. This kiss is nothing like that. His lips are firm, and his tongue moves boldly as it swirls around... my...*' I'm sorry! I shouldn't be laughing, but come on! His tongue moves boldly? Like, all I can think about is a tongue in a Superman outfit! His tongue moves boldly where no man has gone before!

"Okay, okay, okay! It's serious now. Time to get serious. Tongues do not wear capes. This is serious and hot. We're very serious and very sexy. Hold on, I need my spray bottle. Fun fact for you guys. I saw a narrator today at work with a spray bottle filled with water on his stand, and I was so confused. My dad had a spray bottle he carried around the house with him at all times, because Boots, the cat we had when I was growing up, liked to jump up on the kitchen counter and the dining room table. Whenever he'd see Boots sitting somewhere he shouldn't be, my dad sprayed him with the water bottle. I thought maybe we had a cat at work no one told me about. But no. We just have narrators who get dry mouth from all that reading, so they spray water into their mouths."

Sprays water

"Don't wanna get gross dry mouth. Especially since I have gross wine mouth already.

"Okay, we're gonna try this again. Think sexy thoughts, don't laugh, think sexy thoughts, don't laugh...

"*He tastes like peppermint and beer...*' That's an odd

combination. Wouldn't the peppermint overpower the beer? That's like drinking a glass of orange juice after you brush your teeth. That can't taste good during a kiss. The last guy I kissed tasted like eucalyptus, because he had chapped lips and used medicated chapstick. I couldn't feel my lips or my tongue for an hour after he dropped me off.

"Where was I? Oh, yes. *'He tastes like peppermint and beer as he gently... sucks... my tongue into his mouth. His hips... press harder against me and I slide one of my legs around the back of his thigh, until I can feel his... his...'* Oh, God. *'...his... erectionrubbingagainstthethinmaterialofmyshortsbetween-mylegs.'*

"Good Lord. Whew!

"*'His tongue begins to move through my mouth, in tune with the motion of his hips against me. Push. Push. Push...'*"

"I know, I know! I'm laughing. Why is this so funny? It's not funny. It's serious. We're very serious. This couple is dry humping in public. That's serious business. Anyone could walk in on them. How do these narrators read this? You guys! *How* do they read this?

"All right. Hold please."

Sprays water

"Calm down. Think about the neighbor, think about the neighbor...

"*'He pushes his tongue deeper, and slowly grinds himself between my thighs.'* Wow, okay. That's nice. *He takes his time exploring my mouth, and with each jerk of his hips against me, I can feel myself getting… wetter, and… wetter. The throbbing in my… my…'* Rhymes with flit. *'…growing stronger each time the rough denim of his jeans rubs against my bare thighs and his tongue circles mine.'*

"Mmmmmm, that's nice. That's really nice. You know, if something like that would ever happen to me with the neighbor. Which it won't. Because he doesn't see me like that. I'm just the dorky girl next door who can't string together five words when I speak to him. I should maybe move on to the next part of my home-work right now and save these other excerpts for later. I'm supposed to send him a text. How am I supposed to send him a text and act normal when I've got words like grind, wetter, sucks, and rhymes with flit swirling around in my brain?

"It's fine. Everything is fine. I'm fine. Just jump off the cliff and do it already, Heidi. I'm pulling up his contact information. I'm starting a new text… uff da. Why are these buttons so small? Forget it. I'll just use the voice-to-text thing. I'll dictate it into my phone. Easy-peasy.

"Hey, Brent! How you doin'?

"There. My best Joey Tribbiani from *Friends*, even though text doesn't have sound. Whatever. It's simple and cool and flirty, just like my man, Joey. Wait. That's not *at all* what I said, you stupid phone. Could you imagine if I actually sent that to him? Delete, delete.

"Oh, God. Oh no! Please tell me I did not acci-dentally hit Send!"

Chapter 12

"IT'S NOT THAT bad."

"Oh, it's bad. It's really bad," I mutter to Aubrey as I pace around my living room, holding my cell phone to my ear with one hand and biting the thumb nail off my other hand.

Thank goodness she gave me her cell phone number in case of an emergency. This is a code blue situation right now. I'm pretty sure I died of heart failure and now my reanimated corpse is wearing a hole in my carpet.

"Read it for me one more time," Aubrey requests, a hint of laughter in her voice that makes me want to reach through the phone and possibly punch her in the throat.

Who knew wine and bad decisions could make me so angry?

I pull the phone away from my ear and reread the text my stupid phone sent to Brent, where the word Delivered sits right underneath it, mocking me. With a sigh, I bring the phone back to my ear.

"Maybe it's not even his number. Maybe he gave me a fake number like girls do at bars."

Aubrey laughs. "So you'd rather Brent gave you a

fake phone number because he thinks you're annoying, instead of the fact that you sent him the best autocorrected text I've ever heard in my life?"

"Yes!" I shout. "Wait, no. I don't know! Why did I let you talk me into this?"

"Because you're being bold and confident. You drunk-texted him. Big deal. I once sent my father-in-law a picture of my boobs on accident, because his name is right under Jameson's name in my phone."

"Oh my. What did you do?"

"I didn't speak to him for six months, because I was mortified. Are you kidding me? My father-in-law saw my boobs, Heidi. There's no coming back from that. Then one time, we went over there for dinner, and my mother-in-law made chicken breasts, and as soon as she announced what was for dinner, I started choking so hard I almost passed out."

"This is doing nothing to make me feel better," I complain.

"Did you send Brent a picture of your naked tits?"

"No!"

"Then you're fine. You can come back from this. If he doesn't respond, it will be a great conversation starter the next time you see him. *Oh, hey there, Brent! How about that text I sent you? Oh, jeez. Uff da. Wine. Am I right or am I right? Done any ice fishing lately? How 'bout those Twins this season, eh?*" Aubrey says in her best Minnesota accent that sounds entirely too Canadian.

"I don't talk like that," I complain with a roll of my eyes.

"There's a reason why my husband is the actor and I am the writer. Seriously, you have nothing—"

Aubrey stops talking abruptly when the sound of my doorbell chimes loudly through the house.

"Holy shit. Was that your doorbell?" she asks through a loud whisper.

"Holy shoot, that was my doorbell!" I hiss back. I stand in the middle of my living room, staring at my front door like it might suddenly come to life and start eating all the small children on my street, and possibly a few adults.

"It's him! Oh my God, it's him!" she squeals, which makes all the wine in my stomach churn until I have to press my hand there to stop myself from puking all over my carpet.

"There's no way it's him," I mumble with a shake of my head as I slowly inch toward the door. "Why would he just show up at my door at ten o'clock at night?"

"Um, did you read the text you sent him? He probably thinks you have a brain aneurism and he's making sure you're still alive."

"I thought you said it wasn't that bad?" I whisper-scream.

"What kind of a new friend would I be if I was completely honest? When we're old friends, then I can bust out the truth bombs. Wait, what's happening? What are you doing? You can't just ignore the doorbell!"

"Shhh, I'm listening. I have my ear pressed against the door," I reply as quietly as possible.

"What in the fresh hell are you listening for? Don't you have one of those peephole things? Just look out it and see if it's him!"

Oh yeah. That makes much more sense.

Lifting up on my toes, I close one eye and look through the peephole with the other, letting out a gasp when I see Brent standing on my front porch with his hands in his pockets.

"It's him! He's standing on my porch! What do I do?" I hiss, taking a step back from the door.

"Hey, Heidi, you know I can hear you, right?"

The sound of Brent's voice filled with laughter from the other side of the door makes the phone slip from my hand. It drops right on top of my bare foot, which makes my eyes fill with tears as I shout at the top of my lungs.

"Son of a biscuit!"

"I'm sorry! I shouldn't have just shown up like this so late. Just wanted to make sure you were okay."

I can't have him thinking I was yelling at him! Without giving it a second thought, I quickly unlock my door and fling it open so hard it smacks against the opposite wall.

"You betcha, it's fine! Everything is fine! Just dropped my phone on my foot and it hurts like the dickens," I tell him with a big smile. "Why did I say *dickens*? I'm not a ninety-year-old woman. Let's just pretend I didn't say dickens. Oh jeez, I can't stop saying it now. I apologize. I've had some wine tonight."

This makes Brent chuckle, and naturally his dimples make me forget all about how mortified I should be right now. Until he pulls one of his hands out of his pocket, bringing his phone right along with it.

"That explains the text I got from you a little bit ago," he says with a smile, looking down at his phone as he reads my text out loud. "*Dick taste in my palm. Sleazy, sleazy. He bent your dong.*"

Kill me. Kill me right now. Someone please put me out of my misery.

So, it would be bad enough if my phone had only translated **Hey, Brent! How you doin'?** into **He bent your dong.** But no. Of course it couldn't be that simple. I had to go and start recording too early and *"I'll dictate it into my phone. Easy peasy,"* had to sneak its way in there.

Once more, for the people in the back: **Dick taste in my palm. Sleazy, sleazy. He bent your dong.**

"I didn't mean to send you that," I reply lamely.

"Are you sure? It sounds like something you'd say," he tells me with a wink.

Is he flirting with me? What is happening right now?

"I'm a teacher. *Was* a teacher. I'd never have such atrocious grammar in a text. I mean, those aren't even complete sentences."

Oh jeez. Shut up, Heidi!

"I'm sorry," I say. "I didn't mean to bother you so late. You didn't have to come over just to check on me, but thank you. As you can see, I'm good. I might not be able to look you in the eye for the next eight-to-ten weeks, but I'm good."

Brent takes a few steps toward me until he's standing just inside my doorway, with only a few inches separating us. I start thinking about that excerpt I read on my podcast and imagine him wrapping his arms around me, lifting me up against his body, and pushing me into the wall. My entire body flushes and there's a strong tingling sensation happening down there in my general *word that rhymes with flit* area that makes me want to pant like a dog.

I could easily reach up and grab onto his T-shirt, yanking him down so I could kiss him, just like Aubrey did to Jameson earlier at work. Brent *winked* at me. He came over to make sure I was okay instead of taking the lazy way out and just replying to my idiotic text. That's got to mean something, right?

Do it, Heidi. Just do it. Grab ahold of what you want!

"You could never be a bother, Heidi," Brent tells me softly. "And I hope you keep looking me in the eye. You've got beautiful eyes."

Whaaat is happening?

This would be so much easier if it was all happening over text. You know, minus the autocorrect. I could send him the heart-eyes emoji and a thumbs-up. I could take a few minutes to think about what I'm going to say so it comes out all cool and awesome and perfect. But this isn't a text. This is real life and it's happening right now in front of me. I could possibly try to make a heart shape using my fingers and my thumb and hold it over one eye, but that would take too long and probably be weird.

For the love of God, stop stalling and grab his shirt!

Before I can think about what I'm doing, which is absolutely a bad idea going by my recent track record, my hand flies up to latch onto his shirt and pull him toward me. Except my brain is still filled with wine, which then sends a drunk brain-to-text message to my arm, and instead of wrapping my fingers around the cotton material of his shirt, I just punch him as hard as possible in the chest.

Brent winces and his upper body jerks backward with the force of my blow.

"Oh, you!" I giggle a little too loudly, trying to play it off like I meant to do that, wishing I'd never taken that self-defense class my mother guilted me into when I was in college.

I just treated Brent like an attacker and put my whole body into that thing.

Brent laughs and shakes his head at me as he rubs his palm against his chest. I'm trying to figure out if this shake of his head is one that says *You're adorable* or *You're certifiably insane and I'm putting my house up for sale immediately.*

Before I can figure it out, he steps backward out of my doorway and I've lost my chance to grab him and make him kiss me. Actually, that chance flew out the window when I went full-on *Fight Club* on him.

"Don't forget to lock your door. And take some aspirin before you go to sleep," Brent instructs, giving me a wave before turning and jogging down my steps.

"Sorry for drunk texting you!" I shout after him, quickly shutting my door, turning the lock, and gently smacking my forehead against the wood a few times.

As I slowly turn away from the door, I notice my cell phone still lying on the floor where I left it after it dropped on my foot. Bending over, I snatch it up, saying a prayer that Aubrey hung up as soon as she heard the loud clamor of it falling and didn't listen to that disastrous conversation.

"It wasn't that bad!" she immediately chirps as soon as I bring the phone up to my ear.

Chapter 13

*H*AVE YOU EVER had that dream where you're being chased, but it's like your feet are stuck in a pile of mush and you can't move? You keep pushing and pushing and trying to run, and no matter how hard you try, you don't go anywhere. I have that dream all the time, but it's gotten much worse recently. It doesn't take a genius or even Google to tell me what that dream means.

I. Am. Stuck.

I want more out of my life. I want fun and excitement and passion, and I thought I was taking the steps to getting all of that. I got a new job that has nothing to do with teaching. I branched out in my reading and stopped being a prude. I made friends with famous people. I started a podcast. I still only have a handful of listeners who continue to tell me how much I suck every time I upload a new episode, but at least I haven't quit. I've done some fun and exciting things outside of my comfort zone, and yet, nothing much has really changed. I'm still afraid to tell my parents I never want to be a teacher again. I'm still petrified to tell Brent how I feel about him. I'm still walking through a pile of mush, not going anywhere. I'm still waiting for something to happen *to* me instead of going out and getting it for myself.

If last night's interaction with Brent taught me anything, aside from making sure my phone is nowhere within my reach after I've had wine, it's that I need to stop being such a wimp. What if I tell my parents I never really wanted to be a teacher, and they're disappointed in me? What if I tell Brent how I feel about him, and he doesn't feel the same?

I've spent my entire life constantly asking myself *what if* and worrying about the consequences of every potential decision I might make, instead of just doing what makes me happy. If my parents are disappointed in me, it will make me sad, but at the end of the day, that's *their* problem, not mine. If Brent doesn't feel the same way, it will really suck, since we live next door to each other. But that's *his* loss, not mine.

"Well, would you look at what the cat dragged in."

My body jolts in surprise when I hear my mom's voice and I give her a sheepish smile when I see her in the open doorway of their house. Standing on my parents' front porch for the last ten minutes contemplating life probably wasn't the best decision.

"Are you two gonna stand there all day air conditioning the entire neighborhood or are you gonna come

inside and shut the door?" my dad shouts from somewhere inside the house.

"Get in here before your father has a heart attack."
My mom sighs, moving out of the way so I can enter.

It's really no surprise I've come to a point in my life
where I feel stuck. Walking into my parents' home is like
walking into a time warp from the 1970s. This house
used to belong to my grandparents on my dad's side, and
when my parents got married, my grandparents sold it to
them for next to nothing and moved into a retirement
community just outside of town. The only thing my
mom has changed about this house over the years is the
wallpaper. There's got to be at least fifteen layers of
wallpaper in each room. She never rips the old stuff
down; she just papers right over it with something even
more hideous than before. Every room is filled with
some sort of floral design from floor to ceiling that will
make you dizzy if you stare at it long enough. The
kitchen still has the same yellow Formica countertops
and dark brown laminate cabinets. The bathrooms still
have the same little bowl of pink decorative soaps in the
shape of roses on the sink that were there when I was
little that no one is allowed to touch because they're for
"guests," but the guests never use them, because they're
too pretty, so my mom just continues to dust them every
week and puts them right back. I asked my mom once
when I was a teenager why they never upgraded their
house, got new carpet or new cabinets or new anything,

and her reply was, "If it's not broke, why fix it?" She's never been a fan of change. And now here I am, walking in, ready to tell her that her only daughter is changing in a big way.

"It's about time you got here. I'm starving."

I come to an abrupt halt when I reach the living room to find Jameson sitting on the couch next to my dad with a huge smile on his face.

"Peggy, you *have* to tell me where you got those cute little retro, rose-shaped soaps in the bathroom."

Turning around in place, I watch with my mouth dropped wide open as Aubrey comes up to stand next to my mother.

Forget what I said about a time warp. This has officially turned into The Twilight Zone.

"Am I still drunk from last night?" I mutter, looking back and forth between my mom and my new friends.

"If you would have checked your texts this morning, you would've known your mom asked us over for lunch," Aubrey admonishes.

"My phone is currently in a timeout, shoved into the back of my nightstand drawer until it can behave," I remind her. "What is happening right now? Mom, how do you even know Aubrey and Jameson? And how did you get ahold of them to invite them over?"

"I joined The Facebook and sent them a message," she tells me with a roll of her eyes, like it's the dumbest question I've ever asked.

Her face says it all. A stranger might think my mom is smiling and happy to see her daughter, but a stranger would be wrong. My mother's face is clearly looking at me saying, *"Eighteen hours of labor with you, and I had to find out from Sharleen you know famous people. Eighteen. Hours."*

"Her relationship status says 'It's Complicated.'" Aubrey snorts. "I love your mom."

"Heidi's father was on my last nerve when my sister helped me set up The Facebook yesterday. I'm not changing it until he apologizes for putting the empty milk carton back in the fridge. Twenty-seven years of marriage and that man still doesn't know where the garbage can is."

"I'm sitting right here!" my dad shouts from behind me as he gets up from the couch along with Jameson.

"Good!" she yells back at him. "The garbage can is located three feet from the fridge, where it's been for the last twenty-seven years!"

All I can do is stand here blinking as I stare at the woman who birthed me, who doesn't even own a cell phone, because she firmly believes they cause cancer, and who once typed into Google, **How do I Google something?**

I'm still asleep. That's got to be the only explanation for what's happening right now. This is a guilt dream brought on by the fact that I have a new job I have yet to tell my mom about. And if she hears about it elsewhere first, I'll hear about it for the rest of my life. She'll pull it out at a random Thanksgiving ten years from now, just to make sure I never forget.

"Dinner was lovely, Mom."

"Yes, it was. But remember when you lied to me when you were twenty-five?"

If only this could be just a bad dream.

"Since my daughter doesn't care enough to tell her mother about her life and her new friends, what else was I supposed to do but take matters into my own hands?" my mom asks.

"And we're very glad you did, Peggy," Jameson tells her as he and my father join us in the doorway of the living room. "Aubrey and I have been living on takeout and room service. I'm dying for a home-cooked meal."

"Sharleen called me the other day to tell me about how she saw Heidi at work and got to meet a real, famous actor," she states. "And she just went on and on about what they do at EdenMedia. It was a little confusing. She kept talking about the back door. I have no idea about half of what she was telling me. She was still a little loopy from the laughing gas, ya know. So I said to her, 'Sharleen, he's just like anybody else. He puts his pants on one leg at a time like any other man.' Except for Elizabeth Watson's son, on account of how he likes to wear dresses now, but that's neither here nor there. So, who's hungry?"

My dad wraps his arm around my shoulders as my mom leads everyone into the dining room, and he gives me a squeeze as we trail behind.

"You doing okay, kiddo?" he whispers.

"I don't know. Mom has Facebook now. And she didn't go into a twenty-minute diatribe about how my new job is embarrassing and how she'll never be able to show her face in church again."

"Oh, she got all that out of her system with me when she hung up with Sharleen." He laughs. "She's coming to terms with it. She just wants you to be happy. Are you happy?"

I shrug. "I don't know. I'm getting there."

He gives me another squeeze as we enter the dining room before dropping his arm from around me and walking over to take a seat next to my mom.

The table is filled with at least ten casserole dishes, three baskets of homemade rolls, and four Jell-O salads. I watch as Jameson and Aubrey's eyes light up when they see all the food, and my mom tells them to sit down and help themselves. Much to my surprise, it's actually a really nice lunch. My mom doesn't immediately start grilling me about work or tell embarrassing stories about me growing up. We mostly just talk about Jameson and Aubrey and their life in the Hollywood spotlight, and how they try to lead as normal a life as possible.

After we're finished eating and Aubrey and I have cleared away all the dishes for my mom, I make a pot of coffee and bring a tray filled with cups, cream, and sugar into the dining room. When everyone has their mug filled the way they like it, Aubrey quickly excuses herself and goes back into the living room, returning a few minutes later with a stack of books in her arms that I immediately recognize.

Butterflies start flapping around like crazy in my stomach when Aubrey walks right over to my mom and sets the stack down in front of her. The stack of half-naked men covers. My mom has been pretty cool so far this afternoon, but that's probably because my job and what they do there hasn't literally been shoved right in her face. Out of sight, out of mind and that whole thing.

I hold my breath and wait for my mom to shove her chair back from the table and go running from the room to get as far away from those books as possible, hoping to God Aubrey isn't easily offended. Much to my surprise, my mother actually picks up the book on top of the pile, flips it over, and starts reading the blurb on the back.

"Oh jeez, this sounds spicy!" she quips with an excited smile.

"You said you wanted a few extra copies for your friends, so I brought three of each and signed them all. I hope that's enough," Aubrey states.

I couldn't be more surprised right now if my dad jumped up on the table and started stripping.

"You *asked* for her books?" I question, unable to hide the astonishment in my voice.

"Of course I did! Your father and I are supporters of

the arts, Heidi." She purses her lips and gives me an exasperated look like *I'm* the one saying crazy things.

"You still have a velvet painting of dogs playing poker hanging in the spare bedroom," I remind her.

"We're broadening our horizons." My mother shrugs, setting the book down and picking up the next one to study it.

"You do know what she writes, correct? That's a really broad horizon. No offense." I wince, glancing at Aubrey.

"None taken. I write smut. Everyone knows I write smut." She shrugs.

"Don't you dare belittle what you do, young lady," my mom scolds her. "It must be a lot of hard work to come up with an entire story in your head and put it down on paper."

Aaand now I'm back to hearing The Twilight Zone *theme song in my head.*

"I need to get busy cleaning out the gutters," my dad announces, finishing off his coffee and setting the mug down on the table as he gets up from his chair. "Jameson, I got an extra pair of gloves you can use to help me."

"Dad! He doesn't need to help you clean the gutters!"

Sure, I'm friends with the guy, but come on. He's still famous. He walks on red carpets and just did an appearance on *The Tonight Show* last month, and my dad is ordering him to do yard work like he's a neighbor kid from down the street.

"Are your hands broke?" my dad asks Jameson.

"No, sir." He chuckles.

"Then you can help me clean out the gutters. Aubrey, you can hold the ladder," my dad instructs as he heads out of the room and Jameson pulls Aubrey's chair out for her.

"Take a plate of food out to that bodyguard of yours sitting in his car on the curb," my mom adds as I continue sitting there shaking my head.

"Oh, he's fine. He'll eat on his break after he drops us back off at the hotel," Aubrey tells her as she stands.

"The poor man is sitting there just staring at the house. Take him a plate."

"Yes, ma'am." Aubrey laughs, giving me a wink as Jameson grabs her hand and pulls her out of the room, leaving my mom and me alone.

Which I now realize was probably my dad's plan all along.

"Are you mad at me?" I whisper after a few quiet minutes, breaking up the silence in the room that was punctuated only by the ticking of the grandfather clock in the living room.

"Why in the world would I be mad at you?" my mom asks in shock, getting up from her chair and taking the empty one next to me.

"Because I've been avoiding you and didn't tell you

what they do at EdenMedia," I murmur sheepishly.

"Your father and I have sex."

Eew! Not *the response I was expecting.*

"Oh, don't make that look, like you're going to throw up the green bean hotdish you just ate," she scolds. "I might not be hip with the times, but you're an adult and you have to make your own decisions. I can't exactly forbid you from working at a place just because they record dirty books that aren't typically something I'd read. Especially now that I've met someone who writes those types of books, and I think she's wonderful and sweet. I'm sure your dad and I have done all the stuff she writes about, so who am I to judge?"

Again. Eeeeeew! Too much information!

My mother has *never* spoken to me about sex in any way, shape, or form. The only reason she had the talk with me about my monthly visitor was because my cousin Michelle got hers for the first time when she spent the night at our house when we were eleven. I was in the bathroom with her at the time, because young girls do everything together, including pee, and when I saw what was going on, I ran out of the room, screaming for my mom, crying that Michelle was going to die. After getting Michelle situated, my mom pulled me into her room, sat me down on the bed, and said, "Welcome to being a girl. This is what will happen every month forever. Any questions?" Of course I had a thousand questions, but I was mortified. No way was I going to ask my mom *anything.* I learned about sex from secret internet searches and talking about it with my girlfriends. Sex just wasn't something you discussed with your parents. Ever. To hear my mom talking about it so cavalierly right now is insane. Insane and *gross*.

"I'm sorry I didn't tell you right away about Eden-Media and what they do there. I didn't really know how to tell you. Especially since I know you have your heart set on me finding a teaching job," I explain.

"And I'm sorry for making you think you couldn't talk to me about it." She smiles sadly.

"I just didn't want you to be disappointed in me. I know you want me to be a teacher, but...."

"It wasn't what you wanted," she finishes. "Don'cha know I just want you to be happy? No matter what it is you're doing. Unless it's illegal. Or takes you farther than a few hours' car ride away from us. Or involves drugs of any kind. Cindy Carlson's son Billy—you remember him from middle school and when I chaperoned the eighth grade dance and he got suspended for putting vodka in the punch? He started smoking the pot and dropped out of college, and now he lives in Cindy's garage and delivers pizzas. There's nothing wrong with delivering pizzas; it's an honest living, but he's constantly delivering orders to the wrong houses, and Cindy is thinking about doing one of those interventions. Are you smoking weed?"

I bite down on my bottom lip to stop myself from laughing.

"No. No I am not smoking weed."

"Then there's nothing for me to worry about. You do whatever you need to do to bring a smile to that pretty face of yours. Even if you have to do it working in a place where they record P-O-R-N," she says, spelling the word out in a whisper.

I never thought in a million years I'd ever be having a conversation like this with my mother, the woman I thought was incapable of change.

"I can't believe you actually asked Aubrey to bring you some of her books. What are all those Post-It notes doing in them?" I ask, pointing over to the stack she left on her other seat, where all sorts of multicolored pieces of paper stick out between the pages.

"Oh, I asked her to mark all the dirty parts so I can skip over them. I also bought some pretty rolls of contact paper I'm going to cover them with before I give them to the girls," she tells me happily.

Okay, so not everything has changed, but this is definitely a step in the right direction. I should probably take this moment to tell her about my podcast, but I think we've had enough excitement for one day.

"So, tell me about this Brent person Aubrey mentioned before you got here. Is he single? Does he have a good job? What do his parents do? Does he want to have kids? What's his last name? I'll send him a friend request on The Facebook and invite him over for dinner."

Chapter 14

Heidi's Discount Erotica, Episode 4

"**W**ELCOME TO HEIDI'S Discount Erotica, do-do-do! I'm going to try something completely different for this podcast: no wine. I know, I know, it won't be as magical as the other three previous podcasts, but at least I won't make any poor choices when it's finished. Hopefully.

"Anyhoo, I see I have a bunch of new listeners since my last podcast, which is just crazy. I don't know where you're all coming from or why you're here, because honestly, this thing is a train wreck, but welcome! And I'm sorry if you only tuned in because you heard from a friend that some awkward woman does nothing but drink an entire box of wine and then records herself rambling nonsense, mostly about her good-looking neighbor who is way out of her league. Don't worry; there will still be rambling. It's what I do. But for the time being, the wine is safely locked away in the back of my fridge, behind the jar of pickles that is roughly two years old that still has one lonely pickle floating in the juice that I will never eat and will also never throw away, because that's just wasteful, and the Tupperware container that could be leftover spaghetti from three months ago or homemade slime I made for one of my classes and forgot to take to school when I still worked there. The color suggests slime, but it could really go either way at this point.

"Let's see. What's happened since my last podcast a week ago? Oh! Yes! Well, my mom now knows where I work. It went much better than I expected, and she's actually reading some of the books that are recorded at my place of employment. Well, she said she would read them, and she seemed really excited about it, which might be for the best since some conversations with your mom are better left un-had.

"Meanwhile, I know you're expecting an update on my hot neighbor. Well, I don't think I told you guys about how I tried to kiss him and it ended very, very badly. Let's just say, at the end of the last podcast, I sent him a text I shouldn't have. He came over to make sure I was okay, and wine made me go in for a kiss and accidentally punch him. Now I'm back to hiding in bushes whenever I come home and he happens to be outside, because the thought of making eye contact with him again after the last time I saw him makes me want to throw up a little. I spent three hours in my hydrangea yesterday afternoon, and today I have scratches in places no woman should ever have scratches because of that stupid bush.

"Another listener named LoveMyBoo4Ever commented on my last podcast, '*What's the worst that could happen if you just ask sexy neighbor out?*' Um, well, he could say no! He could laugh in my face. And then I'd have to move, and I really, really like my cute little bungalow and the street I live on. I don't want to move. But I also can't live like this. I need to be bold and fearless. My mother knows what I do for a living now, and I didn't spontaneously combust when she found out. I know I won't actually die if I face him again, but it sure feels like it right now.

"Which brings us to today's reading assignment, given to me by my new friend, which will hopefully get me back on the bold and fearless track. Have I mentioned to you guys that she's an author? She's in the middle of writing a new book and gave me an excerpt from one of the chapters she just finished for me to try out. So, here goes.

"*Ahem.*"

*Cough, cough.

"It's fine. I'm fine. I can do this without wine. Just read it really fast and get it over with. Don't think about the wine in the fridge behind the lonely, old pickle and spaghetti slime. It's probably fermented by now and doesn't taste good. Who wants to drink wine that doesn't taste good? Certainly not me.

"*Ahem.*"

*Cough, cough.

"Do you think wine gets sad if you don't drink it? I mean, I know it doesn't have feelings. That's just ridiculous. But when I was little, I had a huge collection of stuffed animals in my bedroom. Probably around two hundred, littering every surface. I remember going to school and almost crying, because I just imagined them sitting on my bed, being all sad and lonely that I left them there and wasn't home to play with them. I swear I could hear their little cries of pain all day long. What if that box of wine is in my fridge, crying? It's so cold and dark in there, and it doesn't understand why I've abandoned it.

"Okay, here's what I'll do. I'll reward myself with one glass of wine if I can get through this excerpt without blushing. That sounds good, doesn't it? Like when I would reward my students with stickers if they did well on a spelling test. I'll just think of this as an adult spelling test

"*Ahem.*"

*Cough, cough.

"'*The delicate scrap of lace from my thong is immediately ripped off of me and tossed to the side. Ryan's... tongue swirls around mine, probing deeper and driving me crazy. I quickly drop my hands to his jeans, ripping open the button and yanking down the zipper, dipping my hand right into his boxer briefs and pulling out his hard, swollen…'* Uh, um… *'…pulling out his hard, swollen…'* Rooster! *'I pump my fist up and down his… length a few times, until he reaches between us and takes himself in his hand, guiding himself to my…'* Flowering lady garden!"

*

*

*

"Uuugh, I'm sorry! Wine time! Folks, I promise I'll study more next time. This is Heidi's Discount Erotica, signing off. LoveMyBoo4Ever, if you're still listening, I'll be in my hydrangea bush until further notice."

Chapter 15

"THANK YOU FOR calling EdenMedia. How may I direct—"

"I told you it was a good idea to bring her a cardigan. It's *freezing* in here. Where's the thermostat? I'm just gonna adjust it a little."

"Peggy, don't touch the thermostat. We have more important concerns. There's a squeaky floorboard. Do you hear that? Rinky-dink construction, that's what this is. Our daughter is working in a place with rinky-dink construction. I need my toolbox."

The phone slowly slips from my hand and I completely forget about the person on the other end of the line as I sit behind the reception desk, watching my worst nightmare come to life.

My parents are at my place of employment.

Oh jeez. My parents are at my place of employment!

Like two tiny yet completely destructive tornadoes, they barrel around the room, adjusting the thermostat, opening the blinds, rearranging the stack of magazines on the coffee table, fluffing the decorative pillows on the couch, rapping a fist against each wall, and complaining about which one is load-bearing and which one isn't.

"Mom, Dad, what are you—"

"Not now, Heidi," my dad cuts me off as he goes back to the squeaky floorboard by the door and starts jumping up and down on it. "You hear that? This needs fixing immediately. The floor could give out at any minute. Someone get me my tools out the trunk of the car."

Please, for the love of all that is holy, let this natural disaster stay contained in the lobby and disappear before anyone knows they're here.

"Yoo-hoo! Is anyone here? I brought lemon bars!" my mother shouts down the hall, holding the pan of her famous lemon bars out in front of her like she hopes the smell will waft toward everyone working today and they'll all just abandon their work and come running.

"Mom! You can't just yell down the hallway at a recording studio," I scold, getting up from my chair with a sigh and coming around the desk to stand next to her. "Everyone is really busy this morning. They don't have time for lemon—"

"Did someone say lemon bars?" Dave yells excitedly as he flings open the door to one of the studios and power walks toward my mother. "Hi, I'm Dave! You must be Heidi's mom."

"It's just a dream," I mutter to myself. "Any minute now, I'm going to wake up and this will all just be a dream."

"Young man, you have a dangerous situation on your hands over here with this floor," my dad informs Dave as he continues to jump up and down on the floor, the squeak of the loose floorboard almost as annoying as my parents being at my work right now.

Dave shoves an entire lemon bar in his mouth while grabbing three more to take with him, pointing his handful of treats at my dad.

"Oh yeah. That thing has been squeaking since the day we opened," Dave says around a mouthful, bits and pieces flying out of his mouth while he speaks.

"Dave, don't talk with your mouth open," my mom tells him, pulling a napkin out of her purse hanging over her shoulder and handing it to him.

"Okay, so it was really nice of you to stop by, but we have to get back to work now," I speak in my calmest voice, keeping the irritation buried deep.

Grabbing my mother's shoulders, I turn her body away from Dave and start gently pushing her back toward the door.

"Don't be rude, Heidi!" she admonishes, stopping in the middle of the room and refusing to move any closer to the door. "Your father and I wanted to see where you work and meet all your co-workers. Where's Jameson? Is he working today?"

"Jameson is *super* busy. Everyone is super busy. To-day isn't a good day. Tomorrow probably won't be a good day either. Maybe Friday five years from now will be a good day. You should come back then."

"Jameson!" she shouts at the top of her lungs, completely ignoring me.

I hear another studio door open down the hall and let out a defeated sigh as I watch Jameson and Aubrey come into view, huge smiles on their faces as they walk toward my mom.

"Peggy! I thought I heard your voice," Jameson says with a laugh, leaning in and giving her a kiss on the cheek before stepping out of the way so Aubrey can give her a hug.

"Jameson, you're not busy right now are you?" my dad asks him as he bounces up and down over by the door.

Squeak, squeak, squeak.

"Just trying to finish up a few more chapters of this audiobook by the end of the day today," Jameson replies before taking a bite of the lemon bar my mom thrusts into his face.

"Good. Go out to my trunk and grab my toolbox. You can help me fix this board," Dad instructs as he bends down to get a closer look at the floor.

"Dad! Jameson doesn't have time to go get your toolbox; he's working. You don't need to fix anything here. I'm sure we have people who do that, right?" I ask, looking at Dave with wide, pleading eyes so he'll help me and get my parents the heck out of here.

"Oh sure. We have a maintenance guy." Dave nods, shoving another lemon bar in his mouth.

Thank G—

"What's his name?" Dad asks with a raise of one eyebrow.

"Don't know." Dave shrugs.

"What's his phone number?"

"Yeah, don't know that either. Jessica used to always get ahold of him if we needed something fixed. Heidi, did Jessica leave you his name and number?" Dave asks.

"We don't have time for that now," my dad complains. "Jameson, go get my tools."

"Sweetie, while you're out there, can you grab the two other pans of lemon bars and the coffee carafe from the backseat? There's also a vase of flowers, a tablecloth, and two lilac-scented candles," mom informs him as she sets the pan down on the coffee table. "This lobby needs some sprucing up. Aubrey, help me move this coffee table over by the window where there's more natural light."

🍷

"AND, THIS IS the break room where we take our breaks. That concludes your tour of EdenMedia, so how about I take you back to Dad and you guys can go home?"

I try to back out of the doorway before my mom gets a chance to walk into the small room and start redecorating it, but it's no use. She shoves right past me and takes a seat at the table. I shouldn't be surprised. A tour that should normally take roughly five minutes, since this is a pretty small building, took over an hour. When I tried to just walk her right by the studios where people were busy recording, she insisted on walking inside and introducing herself, while spending entirely too long scolding the audio narrators on their choice of seating while they record, listing all the ailments they could possibly face without proper back support. She also reorganized the supply closet, convinced one of the producers to stop smoking, made plans to cook lunch for two of the narrators after she gave them a lecture about nutrition when she saw their choice of snacks sitting on a table in their studio, telling them they couldn't touch her lemon bars until they had at least one vegetable, and vacuumed the entire place.

"Mom, we really need to get back to work." I sigh as she makes herself comfortable at the table.

Aubrey accompanied us on the tour, and I quickly shoot her a look that says *"Help. Me."*

She just shrugs. "I'm not here to work. I'm just here to watch my husband work, and to annoy you when I get bored. Sorry. I'm bored." With a laugh, she flops down on a chair next to my mom. They both look at me expectantly. Since my parents have already made enough of a scene this morning—the sounds of a hammer being smacked against the hardwood floor in the lobby, along with my dad shouting orders at Jameson, haven't stopped since Jameson came back inside with my dad's toolbox an hour ago—I figure it can't get any worse. At least Dave didn't fire me when my mom asked him to lift up his legs while he sat at the DAW, so she could get the vacuum under the desk. It's probably a wise decision at this point to keep her contained to the break room until my dad is finished.

Sitting across from Aubrey and my mom, I watch in silence as she hefts her purse up onto the table and begins pulling things out of it. Namely, all of Aubrey's books that she gave my mom when we had lunch at my parents' house a few weeks ago. True to her word, each book has been covered with different floral contact paper so you can no longer see the naked man-chest covers.

"I finished each of your books, Aubrey, and my goodness, you are a wonderful storyteller!" Mom gushes. "The ladies at church read them after I did, and they all want you to come to our next book club meeting."

Grabbing the book closest to me, I flip through the pages before giving my mom a quizzical look.

"Um, Mom? Where are all the Post-It notes?"

She clears her throat, brushes imaginary lint off her shirt, and refuses to make eye contact.

"Post-It notes? What Post-It notes?" she asks, feigning confusion, still brushing absolutely nothing off the front of her shirt.

"The Post-It notes you made Aubrey put on the pages with all the dirty parts," I remind her.

Aubrey is doing her best to smother her laughter with her hand over her mouth, but it's no use. A giggle escapes, and she quickly covers it up with a cough.

"Oh, *those* Post-It notes. Honestly, Heidi, I don't have time to keep track of a bunch of Post-It notes, especially ones that stop being sticky after a while. The wind must have blown them off." She shrugs.

"Really? The wind?" I question, still flipping through the book in my hand. "There seems to be a lot of dog-eared pages in this one. You must have really liked… chapter thirteen, page 127. Let's just see what you liked so much about this page that you had to fold down the corner of it."

My mom quickly snatches the book out of my hand before I can read from the page. Thank God for small favors. Just a quick skim of that page and I saw several references to male and female parts and something about chocolate sauce.

"Oooh, yeah, chapter thirteen," Aubrey muses. "I remember that one now. That was a good one. Jameson and I tested that one out to make sure it would work. You have to heat the chocolate sauce in fifteen-second intervals just to be on the safe side."

"My… *friend* from church figured that out the hard way," Mom says with a sad shake of her head.

"Really? Your *friend*? Which one?" Aubrey asks in

amusement before giving me a quick glance. "You know all your mom's friends, Heidi, right?"

"Just a friend. She's new. Heidi doesn't know her," my mom quickly adds before I even have a chance to silently nod.

"Seriously, what's her name? Maybe I should give her a call and explain the fifteen-second intervals thing to her for future reference. I mean, it is technically my fault I didn't put the proper heating instructions in the book."

"Oh, it's fine! I'll be sure to pass the information along," my mom laughs uncomfortably as her cheeks start to redden.

I *know*. I *know* what's going to happen next, but just like with a train wreck, you can't help but inch a little closer and see what's going on. I could put an end to Aubrey's line of questioning, but a twisted part of me wants to hear my mother admit it. Wants to hear her say out loud that she really liked the books and no longer thinks they're something dirty or something you should never talk about enjoying.

"She could be getting ready to give this thing one more try and she doesn't even know the proper way to do it," Aubrey states, picking her phone up from the table in front of her. "That sounds like an emergency room trip waiting to happen. We should just call her right now."

"Okay, fine!" she shouts. "It wasn't a friend; it was Heidi's father and me. Chocolate sauce was on sale at the grocery store the other day, and you know I can't pass up a good sale. It was buy one get one free. Anyhoo, Heidi's father now has a blister on his pee-pee and he's very sensitive about it, so don't say anything to him."

Aubrey doesn't even bother to cover up her amusement at this point; she just throws her head back and lets the laughter fly. Me, on the other hand? I'm sitting here regretting every decision I've ever made in my entire life that has led me to this point. I just wanted my mom to admit she read the dirty parts and prove to her that these books aren't the work of the devil that no one should ever talk about, not tell me about my father's blistered pee-pee—a phrase I never thought I'd think about in my entire life, and one that will give me more nightmares than the memory of the two of them coming into EdenMedia like wrecking balls.

"Don't give me that look, Heidi Marie Larson," my mother admonishes. "These books have opened up my mind, especially now that I've met the author and she isn't a pervert."

"That's what *she* thinks," Aubrey whispers so only I can hear her, letting out a little snort of amusement at her own words.

I'm too busy being completely shocked about what just transpired in here to find amusement in what Aubrey said. When I was younger and something sexual, or even something closely resembling anything sexual, came on the television, my mother would put her hand over my eyes and start humming loudly until that part was over. I grew up being literally shielded from anything involving sex. And now here my mother is, talking so freely about my father and... chocolate sauce that I have the urge to cover my *own* eyes and start humming until she's finished.

"Well, Heidi, you were looking for an opportunity to tell your mom about that *other thing* you've been doing," Aubrey says through her laughter, giving me an exaggerated wink as she refers to my podcast. "I think this might be the opening you were looking for. Nothing says Heidi's Discount Erotica like a blistered pee-pee."

"Stop saying *blistered pee-pee*," I mutter in annoyance, my stomach churning with the knowledge that I will never be able to look my dad in the eye again.

My mom is looking at me expectantly, Aubrey is just smiling at me like a loon, and I figure, what the heck? Things couldn't possibly get any worse. Taking a deep breath, I blurt it out at once.

"I started recording a podcast, which is kind of like a radio talk show except it's not live, where I just read the dirty parts of romance novels to help me stop being so awkward and shy and gain some confidence with... men."

"And by men she means her sexy neighbor, Brent," Aubrey adds, which earns her the dirtiest look I can muster.

"I thought you two were already dating?" my mother

asks in confusion.

"No! He doesn't even know I exist. Okay, fine. He knows I exist; he just doesn't think of me in that way," I mumble.

"I need to know more about this young man before I can tell you what to do and how to fix it," she states.

"I don't need you to tell me what to do." I sigh.

"What's his middle name?"

"I don't know."

"What do his parents do for a living?"

"I don't know."

"What kind of hobbies does he enjoy?"

"I-I don't know."

"Goodness, Heidi! Do you know *anything* about him?"

"He works in construction. He's really nice. And… um… he, uh, does thoughtful things like mow my lawn and bring my garbage cans back up to the side of my house and stuff. Oh! And he likes lemonade. I know that for a fact, because he always asks for seconds whenever I give him a glass."

Aubrey and my mom just stare at me from across the table like I'm an idiot.

Am I an idiot? How am I supposed to know everything about Brent when I can't even have a conversation with him about the weather without giggling like a preteen talking to the first boy she's ever had a crush on?

"Oh, Heidi. This is just sad," my mom says with a

shake of her head.

Great. My mother, who tried to burn off my dad's you-know-what is sitting here judging me.

"Actually, this could be good. This is the in you need," Aubrey explains. "You just go over to his house after work today and tell him it's time the two of you get to know each other."

"Oh, okay," I laugh sarcastically. "I'll just march right over there and order him to take me out."

"Exactly!" Aubrey says excitedly.

"I was kidding! I can't do that. I'm not ready. I haven't even gotten up the nerve to read anything word-for-word on my podcast yet! I said the words *lady garden* in my last one!"

My heart starts racing and my palms get sweaty as my mom pipes up.

"Lady garden is so 2009, Heidi. I'm with Aubrey. Just knock on his door and take charge!"

Before I can make anymore protests, my dad pops his head in through the doorway.

"Got the floorboard fixed. Jameson was no help. He had to leave halfway through to go record some namby-pamby lady book," my dad mutters in annoyance.

"The correct term is *erotic romance novel,* Henry. Don't make fun of those types of books that provided us with hours of entertainment this past weekend."

My dad shifts uncomfortably from foot to foot in the doorway and lets out a low growl. "Fine. Whatever. Let's go. I need to change my bandage."

Before I can throw up all over the table, my mom gets up from her chair and pats me on the shoulder as she walks behind me.

"Don't worry about his burned pee-pee," she says in a loud whisper. "He'll be fine in a few days. I'll call you later to get all the details about your date with Brent."

Once she's gone and I can breathe again without the threat of my breakfast coming back up, Aubrey gives me a wide smile.

"I swear to God, if you ever write a scene about a burned *you-know-what*, I will never speak to you again."

"I don't know; that might be just the scene to pull you out of your comfort zone and read the actual words that are printed." She laughs.

"This is not funny. None of this is funny."

"You're right. It's not funny that you're a grown woman who doesn't even have the confidence to flirt with your next door neighbor."

"I'm not good at flirting, okay? That doesn't make me a bad person!"

"No, it doesn't." Aubrey reaches across the table and picks up one of the books. "But it's limiting your enjoyment in life." She flips to a particular page before sliding the book over to me. "Read that scene on tonight's podcast. The heroine asks the hero for oral sex. It will help you get some much-needed confidence to ask Brent out after you're finished recording."

All I can do is sit here and blink at her with my mouth wide open.

"It's fine! You only have to say pussy twice and you don't even have to say moist, because I would never do that to my readers."

Chapter 16

Heidi's Discount Erotica, Episode 5

"**W**ELCOME TO HEIDI'S Discount Erotica, do-do-do! I'm just going to be honest with you guys, okay? I'm only recording this podcast right now, because I'm procrastinating in a big way. It's not that I don't love pouring my heart out and giving intimate details about my life to complete strangers. Okay, that sounded sarcastic. I promise I wasn't being sarcastic! Talking to you guys really has been helping. Especially since I can't see your faces and I can pretend like you're not really there. But now, I have to put all this podcast/new job stuff to the test and see if it really has helped. Are you guys sitting down? You should probably be sitting down. You can't see me right now, obviously, but I am coming to you from the floor of my living room. I might be in the fetal position. Who's to say? I might have also snuck a tiny glass of wine. I know, I know! I promised to do sober podcasts from now on, but don't worry. It's just one glass to calm my nerves, nothing crazy. I won't be drunk-texting anyone or making stupid decisions. I will, however, be asking my neighbor out on a date.

"Oh jeez! I think I might be hyperventilating. Or maybe it's a heart attack. My left side is getting numb and I'm a little bit lightheaded. That could be because I'm curled up on the floor on my left side, and hardwood floors are super-uncomfortable to lie on, but whatever.

"I should buy a nice, fluffy area rug for in here. Maybe one with some teal accents to go with the really pretty teal vase on my coffee table that my grandma gave me as a housewarming present... the teal vase I knocked over and smashed into a million pieces when I dramatically flung myself onto the floor an hour ago and my foot kicked the table. It was an awesome vase. A Red Wing pottery vase from the 1930s that my grandmother got as a wedding present and gave to me and I ruined it! It was so pretty with scalloped edges at the top and a soft teal glaze, and I broke it. Maybe I should look into a new coffee table as well. Something smaller.

"Uuugh! Focus, Heidi! You can do this. It's no big deal. He's just a guy. Just a regular guy who likes lemonade. It's like some unwritten rule that guys who like lemonade aren't jerks. I'm pretty sure I read that somewhere. And he *is* a nice guy. It's not like he'll point and laugh at me when I ask him out, right? Right. He won't. Because he's sweet and thoughtful and *really* good-looking.

"Oh no. Now I'm starting to panic again. You guys, he's so handsome it's ridiculous. It's also intimidating. No one should look that good every day. It's not fair. Maybe I could request that he puts a bag over his head while I talk to him.

"Okay, I need to get serious here. My mom has called me thirty-five times since I started recording this podcast to see if I asked him out yet. Oh, and she knows about this podcast now, so that's super-fun. That was me being sarcastic. Thankfully, she replied to a text I sent her earlier by posting the answer on her Facebook profile, because she doesn't understand how technology works. So, I'm guessing the chances of her actually finding this podcast and listening to it are slim to none.

"And that brings me to the romance novel excerpt I've been tasked to read today. Just like the other excerpts, I'm going in blind, and I haven't looked at it yet. Unfortunately, I know what it's about, but it's fine. I'm just gonna go for it, and it will be perfect. So, here we go.

"'*Tell me what you want, baby,* he says to her in a deep voice filled with need.

His hips jerk forward between her thighs, and she feels his hard… his hard… shefeelshishardcockslideagainsther.

'*I want your mouth on my…*' Um. '*I want your mouth on my…*' One word, two syllables, starts with the letter P, sort of rhymes with footsie. *I need to feel your lips and your tongue between my legs. Please, she begs, as his palm slowly glides up her bare thigh. Make me...'* Opposite of the word go.

"Whew! That was kind of hot. And hey, I said a dirty word! You might have missed it, since I said it really fast, but I did it and I didn't die! Wow, this is very exciting. I feel like I can do anything right now. You know what? I'm gonna march right over to my neighbor's house and I am going to ask him out on a date! I'm gonna do it, and I'm not going to be afraid, gosh darnit!

"Okay, wish me luck. This is Heidi's Discount Erotica, signing off."

Chapter 17

"**Y**EAH, YOU LIKE THAT? YOU WANT ME TO COME IN HARDER? OH, I CAN COME IN HARDER. OH MY GOD, PUT YOUR HEAD DOWN AND GET OUT OF MY WAY!"

My fist hovers near Brent's door, when I hear the shouting coming from the other side. Along with a lot of grunting and heavy panting.

"*WILL YOU STOP TALKING ALREADY? I CAN'T FOCUS AND GET THIS DONE IF YOU DON'T STOP TALKING!*"

More loud grunting and some muffled words I can't make out come from inside Brent's house, so I do what any rational woman would do in my position. I move in closer and press my ear against the door. Which is a huge mistake. Brent chooses that moment to start shouting again.

"LEFT TO RIGHT! LEFT TO RIGHT! GOD, YOU SUCK AT THIS! YOU'RE TOO SLOW! MOVE FASTER! I CAN'T FINISH IF YOU DON'T MOVE FASTER! STOP TELLING ME TO PULL OUT!"

I jump back from the door like it's on fire and just burned the side of my face. Going by how hot my ears are right now from what I heard, I'm assuming my ears really are going up in flames.

"WHAT AM I STUCK ON? OOOH, DOUBLE PUMP IS BACK, BABY!"

Oh my word. What is it that I'm currently listening to? I have to say, I've been feeling very empowered lately reading erotic romances novels for my podcast. They're sexy and have such beautiful love stories woven in between the dirty scenes I've grown to love. But this…. I've never read anything like what's happening on the other side of this door. Is Brent into the rough stuff? Is this how that BDSM thing works?

What if he's with Laura Newberg and he finally decided to take her up on her raincheck offer because I've been too much of a chicken to ask him out?

"I NEED SOME WOOD! THERE WE GO! I AM A BEAST!"

My eyes widen so much I'm surprised they don't pop right out of my head. I quickly glance side-to-side nervously, hoping no one else in the neighborhood can hear what's going on in Brent's house. It's bad enough *I* can hear what's going on. Poor Laura.

"Hey, Miss Larson."

"Holy krikey!" I shout as I whirl around when I hear the quiet murmur of my name.

Not only are my ears on fire; my entire face feels like

I just submerged it into a tub of boiling water when I see sixteen-year-old Justin Holcomb standing on the top step of Brent's front porch. I used to babysit him when I was in high school. I've watched him grow into a smart, well-mannered young man who has been mowing my parents' lawn for the last three years. And he just caught me spying on my neighbor, and most likely heard all the unmentionable things being shouted through the door behind me.

"Oh hey there, Justin! How's it going? Are you good? You look good! Boy, it's great to see you. How are your parents? How's school? It's a nice night we're having, isn't it? I was just standing here on Mr. Miller's front porch, because he's got a better view of the... night. That we're having. Which is nice. Isn't it nice? We should go and leave Mr. Miller to his... nice, quiet night, where I'm positive he's having a peaceful evening all by himself."

"I AM NOT GOING BACK IN THERE! YOU ARE TRASH!" Brent shouts from inside.

Because *of course* he does. He couldn't finish his dirty business quietly, could he?

"Okay, well, we should probably go so we don't bother him!" I chirp, quickly moving forward in the hopes that Justin will turn and run before what's happening inside that house corrupts either one of us more than it already has. But, Justin doesn't budge.

"I just gotta deliver Mr. Miller's pizza he ordered,"

Justin informs me, lifting the cardboard box up between us that I didn't notice he was holding.

Seriously? Pizza? Well, I guess all that grunting and shouting builds up an appetite.

I snatch the box out of Justin's hand and toss it behind me, hearing it land with a *thunk* on the porch right in front of the door.

"Pizza's delivered!" I cheer. "Okay, let's go."

As soon as I wrap my hand around Justin's arm to try to pull him with me down the steps, ignoring the shocked look on his face at what I just did, I hear the unmistakable sound of the lock on the door being disengaged and the creak of it opening.

"Heidi?"

As always, the deep, raspy sound of my name coming from Brent makes my stomach flip-flop. But then I remember what a dirty bird he is and tell my stomach to calm the heck down. I really don't want to turn around. As much as I've imagined seeing him half-dressed— okay, fine, not dressed at all—and sweaty, with his hair all mussed up, now that I know the kind of things he's into and what led him to look that way, it doesn't seem so appealing. So, I keep my back to him, because that's completely normal.

"Hey there, Brent! Nice night we're having!" As soon as the words leave my mouth, I want to smack my own face. *He* might be having a nice night, but mine has quickly turned into a dumpster fire. A dumpster fire that no amount of showering will cleanse me from.

I hear him chuckle softly and I roll my eyes.

"Sorry about your pizza, Mr. Miller." Justin shrugs, pointing around me to where I assume the box landed. "She just grabbed it out of my hand and chucked it on the porch. I'm sure it's still good."

Traitor.

All of a sudden, I feel the heat from Brent's body as he steps out of his doorway and stands right next to me, his shoulder bumping against mine. Out the corner of my eye, I see him lean forward and hand Justin some money. I also see that he is *not* half-dressed, nor anywhere near naked. He's wearing a T-shirt and jeans and a baseball cap backward on his head. He looks adorable and not at all like he just gave Laura Newberg the business very loudly and rudely.

"Thanks, man. Have a good evening," Brent tells Justin.

The two of them share a wave, while Justin looks at me like I'm a crazy person before turning and heading down the walkway to his car parked against the curb.

Brent and I stand next to each other in awkward silence as we watch Justin start up his car and pull away. Not wanting to make things even more awkward by talking, I start to move down off the porch, but Brent gently wraps his hand around my upper arm to halt my progress.

"Hey, look at me," he requests softly.

I have no choice but to do as he asks. As much as I want to run and flee from the scene of the sex crime, it would be extremely rude. Especially since he probably knows I could hear everything that was going on. People five miles away could probably hear what was going on. When I slowly turn around, I make the mistake of looking right up into his gorgeous blue eyes instead of just some random spot over his shoulder. My legs turn into jelly, and I open my mouth to explain my presence in his yard, but all that comes out is a tiny squeak.

"Oh my God," he mutters, finally letting go of my arm to scrub his hand down his face, mostly likely trying to rub away the mortification that he knows that I know what he did.

"It's fine! Everything's fine! No big deal! I'm totally not judging you! Whatever you're into is fine with me!"

He lets out a soft, embarrassed laugh and shakes his head at me.

"I swear to you, it's not what it sounded like. Oh fuck. I can only imagine what you heard. I was... a little into what I was doing, and I kind of lost track of—"

"Nope, don't wanna know!"

"Seriously, Heidi. I wasn't.... I'm not.... Here, come with me and I'll show you."

I don't even have time to insist that it's all good, and if he cares about my mental well-being *at all*, he'll just let me run home as fast as I can and forget this ever happened. He grabs one of my hands, laces his fingers through mine, and pulls me across his porch. He scoops up the pizza with his free hand as he moves, stopping when we get a few feet inside his home. I'm so busy calling myself a fool for letting the feel of his hand wrapped around mine make me forget the fact that his sexual appetite is a whole lot dirtier than I ever expected that I barely notice what he's pointing to when we get inside.

A giant, flat-screened television mounted on the wall in front of his couch, paused on what looks like some kind of video game, with cords coming out of it and hooked up to a PlayStation resting on his coffee table in the middle of the room.

"So, this is where I tell you that I'm a huge dork," Brent admits softly as I stare at his set-up. "I'm a twenty-nine-year-old man who spends most of his free time playing Fortnite with teenagers. I know, I know, I sounded like a complete jerk, screaming at them like that, but if you could only *hear* the shit that comes out of their mouths, your head would explode. Those little bastards are vicious. And they beat me every damn time. It's pathetic."

Laughter bubbles out of my mouth, and it takes everything in me not to pump my fists in the air and shout, *"Thank you, Jesus!"* I turn to face him and the butterflies are back, flopping around in my stomach when his hand still wrapped around mine gives me a gentle squeeze. It's then that I notice he's got a headset wrapped around his neck, which would explain why his voice was the only one I heard shouting through the door.

"You must think I am such a loser. I swear I don't spend *all* my free time arguing with kids. I have other hobbies. I like to read, and I like movies, and I—"

"Go on a date with me," I blurt.

I gasp when I realize what I just said and how easily it came out of my mouth. But he sounded so embarrassed and sweet, and I couldn't let him keep going, thinking I was silently making fun of him or judging him or anything. I mean, I *was* judging him, but that was earlier, when I was younger and more naïve. I really feel like I've grown as a person in the last few minutes.

"Okay," Brent easily replies, with a crooked smile on his face showcasing a dimple in his cheek.

"Okay," I repeat, with the biggest, goofiest smile on my face. "So, I'll just go then and let you finish your game and your pizza."

Even though I want to stand here holding his hand forever, I drop it as I start walking backward, our eyes locked together as I go. I feel like walking this way is starting to get awkward, but I've already committed to it, so I feel the need to see it through.

"So, I'll just call you tomorrow and set up a time for our date then?" Brent asks as I continue to back away from him and out onto the porch.

"You betcha!"

I smartly reach out and hold onto the porch railing as I walk backward down the steps, not wanting to look away from Brent's smiling face as I go, because I never, ever want to forget one single second of this moment, regardless of how silly I must look, and like I forgot what it's like to have legs and feet.

"Talk to you tomorrow, Heidi," Brent states, his eyes never leaving mine as he stands in his doorway and watches me walk backward the entire way back to my house.

I finally turn around when I can no longer see him, practically skipping up my own porch and letting myself into my house.

"Holy shit," I mutter to myself as I close the door behind me and flop my back against it, feeling the need to use some colorful language during this momentous occasion.

I just asked Brent out, he said yes, and I didn't die!

"Who knew a little cock would give me so much power?" I exclaim to my empty house.

Wow. That sounded much better in my head.

Chapter 18

Heidi's Discount Erotica, Episode 6

"**W**ELCOME TO HEIDI'S Discount Erotica, do-do-do! I have a date tonight! I have a date tonight! I asked my neighbor out after a very confusing moment where I threw a pizza and contemplated calling the cops. It all worked out, and now I have a bona fide date with the man I've been crushing on for months. I feel so free. And so amazing. My entire body is practically buzzing with excitement, and I'm not nervous at all. Is this what it's like to have confidence? I should have done this years ago. It's outstanding!

"Okay, on to the good stuff. Buckle up, buttercups.

"*His mouth is hot and wet on my clit and he continues the motion and pressure of his tongue as it circles me, realizing that if he changes up what he's doing too quickly, the orgasm that's hovering right there, waiting for me to fall over the edge into oblivion, will slip out of my reach. He pushes his fingers so deep inside me that I feel his knuckles pressing against the sensitive skin of my inner lips. My hips roll against his mouth, his tongue never slowing its assault on my clit, and I bite my lip to keep from crying out. When the tips of his fingers brush against my G-spot seconds later, the first wave of my orgasm washes over me. I squeeze my eyes closed, my fingers clutching his hair as my legs shake and my hips thrust frantically against his hand. I come against his lips and tongue, and he drinks me in, sucking down every last drop and prolonging my orgasm with little flicks of his tongue until my body feels like jelly.'*

"And that, my friends, is how it's done. Boom! Boo-yah! Mic-drop!"

*Thump, thump, thump

*Static, shuffling

"Sorry! I probably shouldn't have actually dropped the mic. That was an excerpt from my good friend, Penelope Sharp. You should read her books. They're hot and awesome.

"Woohoo! Heidi's Discount Erotica, over and out!"

Chapter 19

"**H**OLY SHIT!"

I let out a squeak of surprise as I'm removing my headphones, when I hear the shout from behind me. Turning around in my chair at my dining room table where I set up my podcast equipment, I see Aubrey standing in my open doorway with a shocked look on her face.

I completely forgot I sent her a text a little while ago, asking if she had a pair of black high heels I could borrow. I wanted to look my absolute best for my date with Brent, and ballet flats would not cut it. Especially not with the dress I stuffed myself into.

"You heard that?" I ask sheepishly.

"Every thrusting finger, G-spot word of it! Dude. Look at you being all nasty and dirty and awesome! You didn't even stutter once," she says with pride in her voice as she walks across the room toward me and I get up from my chair.

As soon as I'm standing, her feet come to a stop and she looks me up and down with wide eyes.

"Sweet Jesus, what are you wearing? And what's wrong with your face?"

I nervously try to tug the skirt of the dress down lower on my thighs, but that just makes more of my boobs pop out, so I adjust the top as well. Pull, tug, pull, tug, up, down, lather, rinse, repeat. No matter what I do, this dress is entirely too indecent, and dressing room mirrors should be illegal. It didn't look this revealing when I tried it on at the mall earlier after the salesperson handed it to me and assured me every woman needed a little black dress in her wardrobe. Now that I'm standing here in front of another human being, I'm feeling a cold breeze in places where I shouldn't feel a cold breeze.

"It's a little black dress," I reply with a huff of annoyance when the skintight, strapless piece of clingy fabric just will not stay put over my boobs.

"It's a little black dinner napkin," Aubrey says with a shake of her head, waving her hand in the general area of my head. "What about… this?"

"A very nice woman at the Macy's makeup counter did it. She said electric blue eyeshadow is making a comeback."

Sure, the bright blue powder on my eyes was a bit of a shock when I first looked in the mirror, but it's growing on me. You know, if I don't look in the mirror. I will admit the false eyelashes might be a bit much, and every time I blink, it feels like I have spiders clinging for their lives to my eyelids, but I have to continue on my quest to find the new and improved Heidi.

"Did you bring me some shoes?"

Aubrey's eyes never leave my face as she hands me a pair of strappy black stilettos, and it's starting to make me feel a little self-conscious. I just need to buck up and remember I said *cock* on my podcast. And I asked a man out on a date. None of that was normal for me, but it made me feel amazing. I'm sure I'll get used to the rest of this new me the more I do it, and I'll feel confident and amazing in no time.

Grabbing the shoes from Aubrey's outstretched arm, I hold onto my dining room table to steady myself as I slip each one on. My calves immediately scream in protest, but I read somewhere once that beauty is pain. Since it feels like someone is currently pounding my toes with a hammer, I'm assuming I look gorgeous.

"There. How do I look?" I ask her with my arms out wide, my legs shaking and teetering the longer I stand here.

"Wonderful. As long as you don't try to walk. Or blink. Or breathe. I think I just saw some of your nipple."

"This is exactly the kind of outfit and shoes Laura Newberg was wearing the night I spied on the end of her date with Brent. I'm not sure if she ever got a second date, but this is how she got the first one, so there must be something about it that enticed him," I explain.

"You already enticed him. He said yes, didn't he?

And were you wearing one of your LuLaRoe dresses when you asked him?"

My entire closet is filled with soft, flowy LuLaRoe cotton dresses. Boring dresses. Kindergarten teacher dresses, not sex kitten dresses that will turn a man on. My dresses will just make a man want to do homework. Hence the need for an emergency trip to the mall today.

"Yes, I was wearing a LuLaRoe dress—the one with the alphabet on it, since you asked. Kindergarten teacher clothing. I'm not a kindergarten teacher. I'm a confident, sexy woman who can now say something other than *fern* when referring to the male genitalia."

"Did you just say *fern*?" Aubrey questions as I attempt to walk in a circle around the room.

My knees knock together and my ankles threaten to collapse with each step, forcing me to grab onto anything I can reach as I move, so I don't face plant on the floor.

"Yes, fern," I mutter, my shoulder slamming into the wall when my foot wobbles with a step and throws me off balance.

I quickly grab onto my bookshelf with both hands and hold on for dear life.

"You know how in all those old, classical statues, everyone's privates are always covered with tasteful leaves? Well, my mom always called the penis a *fern* when I was growing up," I explain, slowly removing my death grip on the bookshelf and lifting my arms up in the air on either side of me for balance.

"If this date is a smashing success and you and Brent wind up having sex, promise me you'll shout, *"Give me your fern, baby!"*" Aubrey laughs.

Before I can roll my eyes at her, the doorbell rings. Aubrey looks back and forth between me and the door, neither one of us moving. I'm still standing here with my arms up in the air, because I'm afraid to take another step in these ridiculous shoes.

"Could you possibly answer the door for me?" I ask with a polite smile, trying not to breathe too heavily now that the nerves are back.

I'm pretty sure if I take too deep of a breath, it will completely throw my balance off. I don't exactly want to greet Brent for our first date by being face down on the ground.

"You know you'll have to walk at some point, right?" She snorts as she walks to my front door.

"Everybody likes a piece of ass. Nobody likes a smartass," I remind her.

"Oooh I'm really liking this saucy Heidi." Aubrey grins as she looks back at me over her shoulder and pauses in front of the door. "Put your arms down. Stand up straight. And smile."

I slowly do everything she orders, my body only wavering a little bit.

"Perfect. But I can see your nipple again," she says with a wink before turning around and opening the door.

I quickly tug up the top of my dress, which throws

my stupid balance off and I slam into the side of the bookshelf again, grabbing onto it just as Brent walks through the door.

Oh my word.

Instead of his usual clothing choice of jeans and a T-shirt, Brent has thrown on a pair of black dress pants and paired it with a white, fitted button down with the sleeves pushed up to his elbows, showing off a nice amount of those beautiful, muscular forearms. He looks so good I want to cry. He looks like he just stepped off the pages of *GQ Magazine*, and I look like I let one of my students dress me and do my makeup.

"Hi, I'm Aubrey!" she quickly introduces, giving Brent's hand a shake before moving around him and into the open doorway. "You two kids have fun!"

When she's behind Brent's back, she leans around him and holds her thumb and forefinger up to the side of her head, mouthing the words *call me* before reaching in and closing the door behind her.

Well, this is awkward.

I'm still hugging the bookshelf, and Brent hasn't said a word. After a few seconds of uncomfortable silence, he walks across the room until he's standing a few feet away from me.

God, he smells good.

"Hey there," he says softly, with his gorgeous crooked smile.

"Oh hey! How's it going? You look great!"

His smile gets wider and he cocks his head at me.

"Thanks. You ready to go?"

"Oh sure. I'm totally ready."

It's fine that he didn't return the compliment. I'm sure seeing me like this is just a shock and it will take some getting used to. He didn't expect to walk in here and see Sexy Heidi ready for anything. You know, as long as she has something firm to hold onto.

Neither one of us moves. I'm afraid to let go of my grip on the bookshelf, and *holy cow,* why do women wear these stupid torture devices? I can feel my heartbeat in my toes. That can't be a good thing.

"Do you want to let go of the bookshelf or are we taking it with us?" Brent asks with a chuckle.

"Yep! Letting go right now," I tell him, still not letting go. "Aaany minute now."

Locking my knees as tightly as I can and clenching my thighs until I can almost hear them weeping in pain, I slowly drop my hands from the shelf. Feeling confident I'm not going to fall, I let out a huge sigh of relief as I take a step toward him.

My feet and my legs are clearly over this nonsense, and everything stops working all at once. I tumble toward Brent with my arms windmilling. He manages to dodge my flailing limbs without getting smacked in the face and catches me before I fall. With his arms wrapped tightly around my body and my chest pressed up against his, I forget all about being mortified that I tripped. He's so warm and strong, and I can feel his heartbeat against my chest. I thought he smelled good a few feet away from me, but it's nothing compared to being in his arms. He smells like soap and a hint of woodsy cologne that makes me tingle in all the right places.

Tipping my chin up to look at him, I have to blink rapidly and open my eyes as wide as possible to get these stupid spiders on my eyes to cooperate before I can fully focus on him.

"Sorry," I whisper. "I don't usually wear shoes like this. I'm not quite used to them yet."

The concern on his face softens and he smiles down at me again.

"Did you do all this for me?"

With these shoes, my eyes are at the perfect height to stare right at his lips and watch them move as he speaks. Scenes from romance novels flood my mind, and all I can think about is having his lips on me. Anywhere. My mouth, my neck, my cheek, my elbow... it doesn't even matter. I just want to know what they feel like.

I quickly shake away my dirty thoughts and concentrate on the question he just asked.

"Well, I've been doing a bit of self-discovery lately. Trying new things. Going out of my comfort zone," I tell him with a shrug. "I've seen the type of women you date, and... I don't know, I guess I just... wanted to make sure I measured up."

I wait for him to tell me I look ridiculous and that I

am ridiculous, but it never happens. He just tightens his hold on me and bends his knees a tiny bit to squat down so we're eye-level.

"Are you comfortable right now, in this dress, and in those shoes, wearing a bunch of makeup that you don't normally wear?"

Absolutely. You should keep your arms around me forever and ever.

"No one's ever really comfortable when they try something new, are they? I'll get used to it."

He studies me for a few seconds before speaking again.

"You know how when Hollywood does a remake of a movie, it's never as good as the original?" he asks.

"Um, sure. They should never mess with the original," I confirm.

His eyes soften as they stare into mine and he lowers his voice to almost a whisper.

"Well, I said yes to a date with the *original* Heidi. The adorable, funny, beautiful Heidi who measures so far above everyone else without even trying. If you did all of this for *you*, then I'm fully on board. We'll toss that bookshelf in the back of my truck and have a great evening. But if you did any of this for *me*, it's not necessary. I like you just the way you are."

My eyes immediately fill with tears and I'm blinking so hard to keep them where they are that one of my pet eye spiders decides to dislodge itself from my lid, and it hangs right down in front of my eyeball like it's trying to scurry its way down my cheek.

"My closet is filled with nothing but dresses a kindergarten teacher would wear. I'm not a kindergarten teacher anymore." I sniffle.

"What kind of clothes did you wear *before* you were a kindergarten teacher?" he asks, his arms still wrapped firmly around me.

I let out a huge sigh.

"Kindergarten teacher clothes."

We both share a laugh and I shake my head.

"I just want you to be comfortable when you're with me," he reiterates.

"I would be a lot more comfortable in one of my old dresses, with shoes that aren't trying to kill me, and none of this gunk of my face that looks like a science experiment gone wrong," I tell him, pulling out of his arms to peel the stupid false eyelashes off. "If you don't mind, I think I'll go change."

Brent gives me a smile and a nod as I start to step away, thinking better of it when my legs shake like a baby deer learning how to walk. Brent jerks forward with his arms out to catch me again, but I smack my hands back onto the bookshelf before he can get to me. I quickly remove the death traps called shoes, flinging them to the side and letting out a sigh of relief when my bare feet are firmly planted on the ground.

"I'll just be five minutes. I promise."

"Take your time. We've got all night," he replies as I start walking down the hall toward my bedroom, bringing the butterflies back to my stomach.

At least this time, they're flapping around with excitement instead of nerves.

My mom and Aubrey told me I needed to get to know Brent, and right now, I think I know all I need to about him. He really *is* a sweet, amazing man, who seems to like me the way I am.

I just hope he still likes me if I happen to let some colorful words out. Now that I've let the *shit, ass,* and *cock* fly, there's no reining them in.

Chapter 20

MY INITIAL IDEA for my date with Brent was to take him to a club. Which is partly why I dressed like a two-dollar hooker who did her makeup in a dark closet. Upside down. If the dark closet was on a bumpy rollercoaster going seventy-five miles per hour. I knew Sexy Heidi wouldn't be appropriate for polka dancing at the American Legion, but I figured she'd be right in her element going clubbing.

Do people still call it clubbing or is that not cool anymore? Dance club? Discotheque? Roadhouse?

Since I'm not cool enough to know the answer to that, I had to come up with another idea fast. Something more Original Heidi. Which is why Brent and I are currently on our way to Lola's Lakehouse, one of my favorite restaurants, and only a fifteen-minute walk down the hill from where we live.

With a waterfront deck that runs the entire length of the building, the restaurant overlooks Lake Waconia. Living in the Midwest with all the farmland and flatland, coming to a place like Lola's makes you feel like you're on vacation. It's almost like you forget you live in a small town that most people would call boring, where the air hurts your face in the winter. My family comes to Lola's to celebrate every special occasion from birthdays and engagements to my dad's bowling team coming in first place.

As soon as I suggested walking to Lola's, Brent grabbed my hand and pulled it up inside the crook of his bent elbow, resting his hand on top of mine to keep it in place, and he hasn't let go since.

"I'm really glad you picked the unicorn dress. That one's my favorite," Brent tells me as we walk at a leisurely pace.

I can feel my cheeks flush and I stare at my feet with a huge grin on my face as we get to the bottom of the hill that will take us to the lakefront.

My teal and purple cotton unicorn dress with a scooped neck and capped sleeves is form fitting down to my waist, with a full flowing skirt that stops right above my knees. It's bright and cute and *totally* original Heidi. As is my face. I washed it completely clean of all the gunk then dusted it with powder, some blush, and cherry lip-gloss—the only make-up I own. There wasn't much I could do about my hair that I over-curled, over-teased, and over-hair-sprayed—because that's the only way I assumed women who wanted to look sexy did their hair—other than brush it all out and throw the long black tresses into a high ponytail, also from the Original

Heidi collection. I didn't use the scrunchie that matched my dress though. But only because I couldn't find it.

I've let Brent do most of the talking as we walked, because I'm still afraid of saying something ridiculous, even though I know I shouldn't be. Brent said he likes me just the way I am. And let's face it, I can be quite ridiculous.

"I'm gonna need to know what that sign is all about."

Brent stops both of us on the sidewalk in front of a house right next to Lola's, pointing to a hand-painted, wooden sign in the front yard. The sign reads **If you park here without paying, your car will be towed to Iowa.**

I laugh and tug a little on Brent's arm to get him to continue walking as I give him an explanation.

"So, we have this thing here called Nickel Dickel Day. It's a festival that—"

"I'm sorry; what was it called again?"

"Nickel Dickel Day," I repeat.

"My apologies. One more time?"

"Nickel Dickel—" I stop abruptly in the middle of the parking lot of Lola's when I glance up and see Brent trying to contain his laughter. "Oh my gosh, Brent!"

After I gently smack his arm in admonishment, he finally lets his laughter fly.

"I'm sorry! I couldn't help it. You are just so damn adorable, and hearing you say Nickel Dickel in that accent of yours is the best thing ever and makes it really hard not to kiss you right now."

Oh my God, did he just say what I think he said? If saying Nickel Dickel makes him want to kiss me, I wonder what saying nickel dick would do. Or maybe just nick dick. I'll have to try that out on my next podcast.

"Okay, it's out of my system. Please, tell me everything about this Quarter Dickie Day," Brent says, making me laugh as we continue walking the rest of the way across the parking lot.

"Uff da, it's not Quarter Dickie Day, and you know it!" I scold with a smile. "Anyway, it's a festival in downtown Waconia, with a classic car show, tons of good food, shopping deals all around town, and stuff like that. The sign you saw in that front yard was put there, because some people who have homes close to downtown will rent out their front yards for parking, since it gets a little crazy around here and hard to find a place to park for the festival."

"Okay, I get that. But I don't get the Iowa thing. Why would their car be towed to Iowa?" he asks.

"Let me give you an example. Pretend you're from Iowa, and I'm going to tell you a joke that will explain it all." I clear my throat and give him the biggest smile. "So, hey, do you want to hear an Iowa joke?" I ask him.

"Oh hey, I'm from Iowa!" he plays along.

"Okay, I'll tell it reeeally slooowly then."

I can barely get the words out without giggling, and

I'm pretty sure Brent is just laughing along with me because I'm a dork, and not because he gets the joke.

"So, basically," I tell him through my laughter, "there's kind of this rivalry thing between Minnesota and Iowa. Minnesotans tell Iowa jokes, and Iowans tell Minnesota jokes. And that's why the sign is funny. No one from Minnesota wants their car towed to Iowa, so they will make darn sure they pay before parking in that yard."

"Have I told you recently how adorable you are?" Brent asks as we get to the double wood entrance doors to Lola's.

"Not in the last two minutes. You're slacking, mister."

Look at me, being all confident and joking. Thank you, Heidi's Discount Erotica!

I let go of Brent's elbow as he removes his hand from the top of mine to pull open the door, resting the palm of his free hand on the small of my back to allow me to go in first. My skin feels like it's on fire where his hand is touching me, but not bad fire. Really, really good, tingly fire. The kind of fire that makes me want to ask him to touch my butt.

Oh my God, I feel so scandalous!

Walking up to the hostess stand, Brent requests a table for two, and I quickly ask the woman if we could have a table outside on the deck. She grabs our menus and guides us through the restaurant toward the sliding glass doors that lead outside. Not even the distraction of having to stop every five feet when someone I know calls my name can make me stop thinking about Brent's hand still pressed against my back and how close he stands to me as I make quick introductions, spending a few seconds chitchatting before moving on.

"This really is a small town," Brent jokes as he pulls out my chair for me when we're finally outside, after I've spoken to every person in the room I know.

"It's worse, because I was a teacher. Those were pretty much all parents of my former students," I explain as he sits down across from me, and we both look out at the view of Lake Waconia, the setting sun in the distance creating an orange glow on top of the water, and the sounds of the gentle waves lapping against the deck instantly put me at ease. "Honestly, a lot of people give small towns a bad rap, but I couldn't imagine living somewhere else. I love that I can go anywhere and run into someone I know. It makes you feel not so alone in this great big world."

"Well said. And exactly why I wanted to move to Waconia after living in Minneapolis for a little while when I came here from L.A.," he tells me.

I knew he was from L.A., but I didn't know about the Minneapolis things. I open my mouth to ask him more about why he moved here, when our waitress comes over to take our drink orders, and Brent changes the subject as soon as she leaves. We chat about the current construction site he's working on, and I tell him more about Waconia and other surrounding areas and the different fun things to do around here while we place our food orders and eat our dinner.

All my life coming to Lola's Lakehouse, I would always look around at the couples who were here on a date and be insanely jealous of them. They were having a romantic evening, leaning across the table toward each other, staring into each other's eyes with dreamy smiles on their faces, and I was stuck at a table with my parents while they talked in detail about my dad's bunion.

"I just need to tell you—I can't believe I'm at Lola's Lakehouse, on a *real* date, and not like that time I came here on a date with someone my mom set me up with, as usual, and he left before we even ordered our entrees, and I made up a fake date when the waitress came back and found his seat empty, and I told her my life was in danger," I tell Brent as I take a bite of my beer-battered walleye, no longer caring about trying to impress him by being someone I'm not. I'm kind of a dork. And dorky things seem to always happen when I'm involved. Might as well own it.

Brent pauses his fork halfway to his mouth, slowly dropping his hand back down to the table.

"Yep, gonna need you to elaborate on that." He chuckles.

"My mom set me up on a date with the son of some woman she went to summer camp with once when they were eight," I start explaining as I pop a french fry in my mouth. "They ran into each other last year at Nickel Dickel Days, realized they both had single kids, and decided to ruin both our lives. Anyway, Daniel was a real dud. He was strangely obsessed with birds and did nothing but show me bird pictures on his phone from the minute he sat down. He gasped when I told him I was thinking about ordering the chicken. Daniel excused himself to go to the bathroom after we got our drinks… and never came back. When the waitress came over for the fifth time to ask me if I needed anything, while blatantly glancing at the now empty place across from me, I embellished about my date a little bit. I told her his name was Nicholas Nightingale, and he owned his own private security business and was called away on an emergency for a high profile client. Told her my life had been threatened if Nicholas didn't help out this client, and Nicholas loved me so much that he would risk his own life to save me. Our waitress was a true romantic at heart. I got two desserts out of that little lie to save face, and this place has a chocolate lava cake that is to die for. Plus, Nicholas Nightingale didn't turn into a huge disappointment, like every other date I've been on."

Man, way to be a Debbie Downer, Heidi.

"The only way this date is going to turn into a disappointment is if they're out of that chocolate lava cake you just mentioned. I might flip a few tables." He shrugs easily, digging back into his dinner.

I love you and I want to have all your babies.

The rest of dinner is easy-going and perfect. There's never a lull in conversation, and both of us laugh so much that I'm sure my cheeks and stomach are going to ache tomorrow. After we both get the chocolate lava cake, Brent agrees that it is to die for, pays the check, and holds my hand as we're walking back out through the restaurant. I don't know what we should do next, but I know for sure I'm not ready for the night to end. I'm so ridiculously giddy I can't even stand it.

"Brent, is that you?"

My head jerks up as we get to the front door and find Laura Newberg standing there. Laura Newberg wearing a teeny, tiny black dress she isn't constantly fidgeting with, standing tall in black stilettos without a wobble in sight.

She struts confidently over to us, doing a double-take when she sees me, her mouth dropping open when she looks down and notices Brent and me holding hands.

I immediately yank my hand out of his, trying my hardest not to compare myself to the blonde bombshell standing in front of me, especially after what Brent said to me back at my house and what a great dinner we just had.

"Heidi! Oh, it's so good to see you!" Laura exclaims happily, quickly throwing her arms around me and giving me a big hug while I stand there stiffly with my arms down at my sides, in complete shock.

"I didn't know you two were dating! You are just so adorable together. I can't stand it! Brent, you treat this girl like a princess, you hear me? She is an absolute sweetheart!"

Oh, I am the worst human being in the world for thinking so badly of Laura when I saw her that night in Brent's yard.

I thought for sure I was about to have my first chick fight, and now that I know my eyes aren't about to be clawed out, and with a quick look at Brent to see that he's staring right at me and not even glancing in Laura's direction, my confidence quickly comes back.

Before I break down in tears like a big baby, I fling my arms around the woman and give her another hug, turning my head a little to whisper in her ear.

"Thank you for the blowjob thing. It's all because of you that I freed the cock."

I pull back with a huge smile on my face, while Laura stares at me like I've lost my mind.

"Okay, well, you two have a good evening."

As soon as she walks away, Brent grabs my hand again and laces his fingers through mine as we walk out the front door.

"I'm sorry, but was that weird? We only went on one date. I didn't realize you two knew each other."

"Nope, not weird at all," I tell him, and I actually mean it.

He's with me tonight, not Laura, or someone like Laura. He's with *me*. Dorky, adorable, original Heidi.

And he still wants to hold my hand. And he isn't running away. And he's smiling at me with that sexy dimpled smile, and he's asking me what we should do next, and I'm back to being so giddy I can't stand it.

"I have an idea what we could do next, but we're gonna need to drive there."

"THIS IS SO fucking cool," Brent says, staring across the street in awe.

I decided to end our evening at another one of my favorite spots, Paisley Park. It used to be the artist Prince's private estate, and sadly, it's where he died. It's since been turned into a museum and is open to the public. Technically, we're not on the actual grounds of Paisley Park, because it's 9:00 p.m. and the museum is closed. We parked, and Brent pulled a blanket out of the backseat of his truck, spreading it out on an empty, grassy area across the street from the museum. We're sitting side-by-side with our shoulders touching and our legs stretched out in front of us, staring at the massive white structure across the way, which is lit up with purple lights, almost making it look like the sky above it is glowing purple.

"So, why did you move here from L.A.? And why didn't you stay in Minneapolis?" I ask after we spend a few quiet minutes staring at the lights.

"Going right for the deep stuff, huh?" he asks with a soft laugh.

"If you don't want to talk about it, that's fine."

He bumps his shoulder against mine and gives me a reassuring smile.

"I'm just kidding. It's weird. I feel like I've known you forever, and we've talked a bunch of times since I moved in, but not about anything important. I'm just going to warn you; this will sound way more dramatic than it actually is."

"Oh jeez. Are you on the run from the law or something?"

He shakes his head with a laugh. "Seriously, stop being adorable. I cannot be held responsible for my actions if you don't stop."

I lean back and wait for him to continue, trying to be as un-adorable as possible.

"So, yeah." He sighs. "I moved here for a woman. Someone I had been dating for about a year back in L.A. We both worked for the same bank, and she was asked to transfer to Minneapolis to be a branch manager. So, I requested a transfer and went with her."

"Wait! You were a banker? Like, you wore a suit and tie to work every day and crunched numbers at a desk?" Before tonight, I'd only ever seen him in ratty jeans and T-shirts, always comfortable with working outside and being dirty and sweaty, so I just assumed it's what he'd always done.

"Yep. I was a nine-to-five corporate man. It wasn't until we moved out here into a high-rise apartment in downtown Minneapolis that I realized how miserable I was," he tells me. "I lived in a suburb of L.A. Close enough to the hustle and bustle of the big city, but far enough away that it was quiet and peaceful when I needed it to be. Living right in the middle of the city, with all the noise and chaos, just didn't make me happy. I quickly realized working in a bank didn't make me happy anymore either. I took a road trip one day to clear my head and stumbled across Waconia. I loved everything about it. When I tried to convince Megan to move out here, she wasn't having it. She couldn't survive without a twenty-four-hour concierge or a Starbucks within throwing distance. That was when I realized *Megan* didn't make me happy."

"I'm so sorry," I whisper.

"I'm not. We weren't right for each other. She wanted to be with someone who enjoyed constant pampering just like she did, and that's just not me. When I told her I quit my job and one of my friends from back home who owns his own construction company got me a job out here, I thought her head would explode. We ended things, I bought the bungalow next to yours, and now I get to work outside during the warm months, and snowplow in the winter months, and I've never been happier. Sometimes, you just have to take a chance. Life is short. Why should you spend it being miserable? Plus, if I was still a banker in Minneapolis, I wouldn't be here with you right now, looking out at a purple sky."

He's staring across the street at Paisley Park, and I'm staring at his profile, wondering if I could safely perform one of the maneuvers in a book I read. Something about straddling the guy's lap and kissing the heck out of him. Brent's head slowly turns to face me, and our noses are just a few inches apart. My heart is beating rapidly in my chest as I try to remember all the mechanics of the scene I read, like where to put my hands, and do I have to stand first and then just sort of squat over him before plopping down on his lap? And is it customary to warn someone before you do something like that or do you just jump right on him? Everything I read is swirling together in my head until scenes start getting mixed up, and fingers are going in ears, and tongues are licking eyebrows, and I start to panic that I'm going to completely screw this up.

"You look way too serious right now. Quick, tell me the craziest thing you've ever done, so I don't feel like an idiot for spewing all of that just now," Brent pleads.

I think of my podcast, but there's no way in heck I'm telling him about that right now—or ever.

"So, when I was student teaching, one of our arts and crafts projects was to make something the students loved out of a paper plate, and then we'd hang them around the classroom as decorations," I speak quickly. "One of my students wrote 'I love pussies' in big letters on his plate. I asked him whatever he meant by writing such a thing, and he told me he loved pussy cats. Well, I couldn't very well display his work. So while it was drying, I snuck it into the bottom of the garbage can and told him it must have flown out the window. The poor kid was distraught, but to this day, I stand by my decision to destroy a child's artwork and lie about it. Not that there's anything wrong with the word he used, but there's more than one meaning for it, and one of those meanings is completely inappropriate for his age level."

I blow out a huge breath of air when I'm finished, my nerves not quite as shot as they were a few minutes ago. Glancing over at Brent, I see him sitting there with a huge smile on his face, shaking his head at me.

"Never, ever change, Heidi Larson," he tells me.

Chapter 21

Heidi's Discount Erotica, Episode 7

"**W**ELCOME TO HEIDI'S Discount Erotica, do-do-do! I'm a little bit in shock right now, and not just because I had the most amazing date in the history of dates last night, but because it looks like I now have a few thousand new listeners! I'm going to assume my friend Penelope Sharp might have mentioned it to her readers—so hi, Penelope Sharp fans! I don't know whether to thank her or spank her. Oh! That was dirty and I didn't even mean for it to be. I'm going to try to not be nervous that there are so many of you out there listening to me ramble.

"Just to give you a quick update on the whole 'finding the new me' thing, it seems to be going well. I'm starting to realize I don't need to completely change who I am as a person, on the outside or on the inside. Some people like me just the way I am. I just want to be...

more. I want to be a three-dimensional person. I don't want people to look at me and only think, 'Oh, she's so cute.' I want them to look at me and see lots of things. Things about myself I never even felt before now. I want them to see someone who's strong, confident, sexy, bold, and fearless. And I want to feel those things within myself as well. I'm getting there. Slowly but surely! And just between you and me, I think my neighbor is going to do a bang-up job helping me get there.

"Oh! I said bang! I didn't mean it like that! Wait, maybe I did. I'm just out of control!

"Speaking of my neighbor, like I said, our date was amazing. He was amazing. What wasn't all that amazing was that it ended with a kiss. On the cheek. There was all this crazy tension as we stood there on my front porch at the end of the night, just staring into each other's eyes, and I thought for sure he would do it. Sadly, no. My friend told me I should have just grabbed his shirt, yanked him to me, and laid one on him. Which of course made me immediately call her crazy. But she's right. I could have taken charge of the situation and taken what I wanted, but I didn't. Because I was scared. Because cute, one-dimensional Heidi is still in there somewhere screaming, 'Oh, my God nooo! What if he laughs at you? What if you suck at kissing and he makes fun of you? What if what happens the night you drunk-texted him happens and you punch him again?'

"No more being scared allowed! I'm putting my foot

down. Which brings us to my next exercise. Ladies and gentlemen, I give you Heidi's Dirty Dictionary! I will go through the alphabet coming up with as many dirty words as I can, so I can get them all out there in the world and practice just breaking the rules. So, don't hold it against me. I know you probably know most of these words already, and might even use them daily. Good for you! Oh, if there are kids around, which I really hope going by the name of my podcast there aren't, but still, if there are kids in your general vicinity, it would be super if you just... send them outside or something. Whew! Here we go.

"A is for... ass. Or asshole.

"B is for... I was gonna say butt. That won't do. Ummmm, B is for boobs. Breasts. Balls. Oooh, boner! That's a good one.

"C is for cock. And, you know, the word that rhymes with... punt. Oh! And climax! Yeah, that's a good one. That's a reeeally good one... I almost did that last night after all the sweet things my neighbor said to me, and the way he looked at me, and how good he smelled."

*

*

*

"Sorry, where were we? Oh yes, D.

"D is for dick.

"E is for... erotic. Yeah, erotic! All I could think of at first was egg, but that's not dirty. Unless you're talking about the birds and the bees, but yeah. Not dirty. Very clinical. Okay, moving on! This is so easy!

"F is for, well, fuck, obviously. Oh my God, I can't believe I said that! Wow, that's super fun to say! I'm just gonna say it again. Fuck! My, it's fun to shout. Okay, what else? Well, fornicate. Fellatio, I know that one. But that's more scientific, so I don't know if it's dirty or not. Let's test it out. I would like to perform fellatio on you. Nope. Not feeling that one. Moving on.

"G is for…. Gosh, what would G be for? Grinding? Yeah, grinding.

"H is for… hop on my lap? No, that won't do. My goodness, I take back what I said about this being easy. This is hard. Oh! Hard! Yep, that works. H is for hard.

"I is for… inside. As in, he buried himself deep inside me. Oh wow, that's spicy!

"Okay, J is for juicy. Yeah, that's good. I mean, J is also for… no. I'm not gonna say that. You know, the stuff that comes out of the guy's… yeah. That's not at all appealing to say.

"K is for kinky.

"L is for… laaabia? Is that sexy and dirty? Do women say, "Oooh touch my labia"? Probably not. How about lust? That's better. L is for lust.

"M is for masturbate. Or mount. I saw that in a book once, so it must be dirty.

"N is for… nookie. No, that's not dirty. Oh! Necrophilia! Wait, that's too dirty. And illegal. N is for…

narrow space between my legs.

"O is for orgasm. Or another one that goes with that would be O face. Like, what's your O face when you orgasm. Oooh, O is for oral. Yeah, that's nice. That's a good one.

"P is for penis. But again, I don't think that's very dirty. P is for... pussy.

"Q is for quickie. Which, in my experience, wasn't all that sexy. Or fun in any way. But I've read that if done right, it can be very satisfying. I will hold my judgment for now.

"R is for... um, riding? Riding.

"S is for schlong. S is also for... slit?

"T is for twat. T is also for tunnel. I've seen that one in books. And tongue. But I think it's dirtier if you use it as a verb. Like... he tongued me. Oh, I hope my mother never listens to this.

"U is for... Uranus! No, I can't say that. That's not a good one. All I can think is uvula. But that's like, at the back of the throat. Oh! Well, all right! That works when combined with O is for oral.

"V is for vagina, obviously. But I don't think they use that in those books very often. Vulva, maybe. See? I keep coming up with doctor words. It needs to be dirty. What about voracious? She has a voracious vagina. Oh jeez! Now I can't stop thinking about a vagina with teeth, eating everything in its path. Okay, I need to move on.

"W is for wet, and want.

"X is for X-rated.

"Y is for…. What would Y be for? Y could be for yes. You read that a lot in those books when things are happening. Like, yes, yes, yes!

"Z. I think Z is going to be a wash. No wait, Z is for zipper, which he pulled down to free his hard length from its denim prison. Darn, I'm getting good at this.

"So, okay! I said some dirty things, and it's good practice. Maybe it will help me get a kiss on my next date with my neighbor.

"This has been Heidi's Discount Erotica, signing off!"

Chapter 22

"**A**RE WE REALLY arguing over this right now?"

The corner of Brent's mouth is tipped up in amusement as I stand facing him, in front of the Ferris wheel at the Minnesota State Fair, with my arms crossed in front of me in a huff. Tons of people are pushing their way around us, and we're causing a bit of a traffic jam just standing here in the middle of the midway not moving, but I don't care. The midway is the section of a fair where all the rides and game attractions are located. It's the most popular part of a fair, tied for first with the food area. When I say it's flooded with people, it's *flooded* with people.

Again, I don't care. This is too serious of a discussion to have while walking in search of our next fair food item.

"Yes, we are most certainly arguing over this right now. We are in our first fight," I inform him.

"On our second date," Brent replies, the corner of his mouth twitching so hard that his infuriating dimple pops out.

He takes a step toward me until we're toe-to-toe, and I have to tilt my head back to look up at him. His chest brushes against my folded arms, one of his hands reaching up and pressing gently against my hip.

Oh my. He's so dreamy. No, no, no. I can do better than that. He's so… fffucking dreamy. Wait! I'm mad at him. We are in a fight. He's doing this on purpose to distract me. Oh no you don't, mister!

"Well, it had to happen sooner or later," I tell him, my voice rising as the loud buzzing and clanging bells sounding right next to us at a game booth announces its current winner. "Might as well nip it in the bud now."

I try my hardest to keep a stern look on my face as I look up at Brent. He keeps his features schooled, and we are currently vying for first place in a serious staring contest. Which doesn't last long at all. Both of us suddenly burst out laughing at the same time. My hands automatically unfold between us, and I press my palms against his chest.

Oh! He's got a nice chest. I can't believe I just put my hands here like it was no big deal! The power of the F-bomb is with me.

Brent shakes his head at me with a smile, neither one of us paying attention to all the people and noise around us.

"It's called soda," Brent informs me with mock-haughtiness.

"Brent Miller, for the last time, it's pop! It's only called soda if you live in the 1950s and you're at the malt shop, drinking from a soda fountain. Do you really want to start our first fight all over again, when we were just about to have our first make-up?"

His hand on my hip slowly slides around my side and across my lower back, pulling me snuggly up against him.

My fingers curl in until I suddenly realize I'm gripping his T-shirt in my hands.

Just yank his face down to yours and kiss him! Who cares if you're surrounded by hundreds of strangers? No one! Do it!

"Our first make-up, huh? What exactly did you have in mind?" he asks, the tips of his fingers starting to make these gentle swirling motions against my lower back.

I have kissing this man in mind. And in my heart. And in my stomach. And waaay down south, if you know what I mean.

"We could go down south!" I immediately quip, my mouth dropping open when I realize what I just blurted out. "I mean, not south as in Florida. That would just be crazy! And definitely not south as in the place where the ferns are. You know what? I'll just stop talking now."

Brent's smile never leaves his face, and it's not one of those smiles most people give me when I say something weird. The smile that is more fake than real, because they don't want to hurt your feelings by making you think you're weird, because that's the Minnesota way. Brent's smile is so genuine when he looks at me. I make him laugh with the things I say. But he's not laughing *at* me. He's laughing *because* of me. He's not immediately heading for the hills every time more of my weirdness comes out. Dare I say, he might even be a little turned on by my weirdness?

Brent's arm tightens around me, and we're so smushed together I can feel every inch of him from his chest to his thighs.

Oh. Oh! Oh my. He's turned on by my weirdness! He's turned on by my weirdness! I. Can. Feel. Every. Inch. Of. Him. H IS FOR HARDNESS!

"Heidi Larson, stop making out on the midway!"

I jerk away from Brent's body so fast I slam into someone walking by us, quickly apologizing before turning around to glare at the person who just… cock-blocked me.

"Aunt Margie, it's so nice to see you!"

I smile at my aunt, but I'm really hoping my eyes are conveying just how annoyed I am with her right now.

"Are you having a stroke? What's wrong with your eyes?" Aunt Margie questions. "And who's the hottie behind you I almost had to spray with a hose?"

Brent might be totally on board with *my* weirdness, but when you add my family to the mix, that could be his breaking point. I guess we might as well find out his true character right from the get-go, before I fall even harder for him. One dose of my aunt can break even the strongest of men.

Godspeed, good man.

Brent moves to stand next to me, sliding one arm around my waist and holding his free hand out toward my aunt.

"Brent Miller, ma'am. I live next door to your niece."

Aunt Margie shakes his hand, clasping her other hand on top of his to hold it in place when he tries to pull away.

"So, this is the sexy neighbor you've been going on about. Oh, you betcha, I see the appeal!"

"I haven't been going on about anything." I laugh nervously, turning away from Brent's amused smile to glare at my aunt. "I have no clue what you're talking about."

"You know, that tape recorder thingy you're—"

"Oh hey there, Christie!" I shout, cutting off my aunt to lift my hand and wave at absolutely no one I know behind her.

I'm pretty sure I don't even know anyone named Christie.

"Christie Nelson's here? She just fractured her ankle on her mail route yesterday and isn't supposed to be walking. Is she in a wheelchair? Where is she? Christie!" my aunt shouts as she drops Brent's hand, turns, and looks all around.

Crap, I really stink at this. Maybe some F bombs would work. Ffffuck. Fuck! Okay, much better.

"Looks like Christie's already been swallowed up by all the people. We should probably get going. Brent's got a lot of things left to eat that are on a stick and deep fried," I tell my aunt.

I am in no way ready for Brent to know about my

podcast. It's too soon! He'll think I'm a psycho. I know I should be all confident and own it, because it truly has helped me get where I am right now, but oh my God, the things I've said about him! All the dirty words I've said! Nope. Can't tell him. Not right now, but I will. There's no way I could keep something like that from him forever. I'll tell him sometime in the very, very distant future. Like, say, our fiftieth wedding anniversary, when he's old and frankly just too tired to leave me because it would be too much work to argue about who gets the leather sectional and who gets the tiny spoon collection from all the states we visited on all the vacations we took together.

"Oh sure!" Aunt Margie nods, immediately taking to my gentle suggestion that she needs to go away. "I have to get back to your Uncle Harold in the 4-H building. He got to talking with one of his poker friends, and I left them to it to go get my cheese curds." She smiles over at Brent as she walks up to him and pats him on the shoulder. "It was nice to meet you, sexy neighbor. My niece is just the cutest. You two look great together. Don't screw it up."

With that, she walks away from us and disappears into the crowd.

"So, now you met my family. Obviously, you can see where I get all this normal from," I tell Brent, using my hands to gesture from my head down.

He grabs one of my hands, pulling it up to his mouth

and placing a soft kiss on top of it.

"Normal is overrated and boring," he says, lacing our fingers together and turning us around to start walking with the flow of traffic. "We need to get a move on. I have to find those cheese curds your aunt mentioned."

$$\text{\textyen}$$

"ALL RIGHT, TELL me what's wrong," Brent states, my hand pausing on the door handle of his truck after he parked and we both unbuckled.

"Nothing's wrong. Why would you think anything is wrong?"

"You've been a little... off. Ever since right around the time we walked away from your aunt."

I can't believe he even noticed that. It's not like I was pouting or frowning or anything after we walked away from her. I really did have an amazing rest of the day with him. One of the best days ever. Big City Brent was completely at home at the fair. He tried every strange food on a stick I gave him, pet every animal, rode every ride, and looked at everything in the exhibit barns, all while happily carrying around his free yardstick from a local gas company and fanning himself with his free flyswatter from a local homebuilder. He put his arm around my shoulders and I rested my head in the crook of his neck when we rode the Ferris wheel, and he carried all the stuffed animals he won me playing games.

But no matter how amazing the day and evening was, and no matter how much I laughed, there was still something nagging at the back of my mind, and Brent noticed.

He rests his arm along the back of the seat and his other hand on the steering wheel as he turns his body to face me. I turn toward him as well, pulling my left leg up and resting the side of my knee on the seat so I can fully face him.

"My aunt called me cute," I tell him.

He continues looking at me, the soft glow of the lights on either side of his garage door illuminating the inside of his truck enough that I can see the curious expression on his face.

"Okay. And that's a bad thing?"

"All my life, I've been called cute. *'Oh, you're so cute!' 'Isn't she cute?'* This guy named Pugsley and I were named cutest in our high school class. Not most likely to succeed, not most musically talented or most athletic, or best looking… cutest," I explain with a sigh. "Now, I know it sounds ungrateful to complain about something that people usually mean in a nice way. I do have freckles in the summertime, which made my dad call me *cute nose* all the time. And I suppose being cute has gotten me out of detention and a traffic ticket or two, which is probably unfair, but hey, you use what you got, right?"

Brent laughs softly and nods. "I'm with you so far."

We both lean in a little closer to each other as I continue.

"Just hear me out. When I'm in a group of people and I speak up to share an idea or add a story to the conversation and other people say, 'Oh, isn't she cute?' it feels like I'm a puppy getting patted on the head. It's like the Minnesota Nice version of shut up. That's one of the only things I loved most about being a kindergarten teacher. To my kids, I was funny, nice, and also sometimes strict, in charge, someone they turned to because I knew things about the world. They never once called me cute, and you know what? Even when I thought *they* were cute, I would try to praise something else, something specific, something they could *do*, not just 'being cute.'"

Brent slides closer to me on the bench seat until our knees are touching, leaning in even more until his face is only a few inches away from mine, not saying a word, just listening, and letting me get all of this out.

"And when I had crushes on guys and I found out through the grapevine that they thought I was cute? Kiss. Of. Death. Because I heard those same guys talk about other girls in our class, after the girls passed by in the hall, or finished a class presentation or a cheerleading routine. They'd say, 'She's so hot!' doing anything they could to make that girl notice them," I continue, talking faster and getting slightly more passionate—also known as loud and annoyed—with every word. "Like Kirsten Hanson, whose default expression was always like she'd just smelled a fart. Boys tripped over themselves to get her to acknowledge their existence. Is that what guys want? Some snobby girl who acts like she hates everybody? I didn't know what to do with that information. I wasn't a snobby girl. I was dorky and talked a lot, when I wasn't being nervous and shy and awkward. I just don't want to be treated like a puppy, you know? I'm more than that. I'm more than just cute."

When I finally run out of steam, I realize Brent's hand, which was resting on the back of the seat next to me, slid over my shoulder and up around to the back of my neck while I was talking. He's looking at me so seriously right now that it's making me nervous.

"When I tell you you're adorable, I hope to God you know I am not patting you on the head. It means you make me happy, you make me laugh, and you make me want to be a nicer person," he tells me with conviction, his hand tightening slightly on the back of my neck, inching my face closer to his. "When I tell you you're adorable, I'm telling you I *notice* you. From the minute I moved in next door, I noticed you. I know you're more than cute. You're beautiful, smart, funny, and sexy. You're someone who knows what she wants and goes for it."

He's giving me a hint, right? This is a hint? Oh shit, hell, damn, dick! Please let this be a hint.

"I do know what I want," I tell him firmly, my eyes trailing down to stare at his lips.

"What do you want?"

After a few seconds of staring at his mouth, my eyes move back up to his and I swallow thickly, pushing the nerves away.

"To kiss you," I whisper.

He smiles.

"So, kiss me."

Without giving it another thought or moment of worry, I grab onto the front of Brent's T-shirt and pull him the rest of the way to me, tipping my chin up and pressing my lips to his.

Chapter 23

Heidi's Discount Erotica, Episode 8

"**W**ELCOME TO HEIDI'S Discount Erotica, do-do-do! I'm so sorry it's been a few weeks since my last podcast. I read all your comments on my website after my last one, and you guys are just so sweet checking in on me! Someone asked if I had an address they could send something to, and at first, I was just going to throw it out there, because this is Waconia and I know pretty much everyone. But oh jeez, there are a lot of you listening now! Last time I checked, I was up to four thousand listeners. This is just so crazy!

"Anyway, I'm pretty sure you're not all from Waconia or I'd probably be banned from church on Sunday. Penelope suggested I get a post office box for listeners to send me things. So, I did it! And I already got my first piece of mail. Someone who didn't leave their name on the envelope sent me a very nice, laminated card with a ton of different words for penis. It's the most amazing thing I've ever seen. Who knew there were so many words? I'm hoping if I read this thing for you guys out loud, it will give me some more magical powers of confidence.

"I'm happy to report that I have kissed my neighbor. Lots and lots of kissing my neighbor has been happening the last few weeks, which is why I haven't had time to record any podcasts until now. But, here's the thing. He told me he thinks I'm sexy. He said the words to me and I heard them, and they made me feel good. But I'm always the one who makes the first move. Which is great that he's letting me have control and show him I can be confident and take what I want, and he definitely seems to be enjoying himself, and it turns out I'm not a bad kisser. I guess I just want to really believe I'm sexy. Believe it deep down in my bones. I don't want to just act sexy; I want to *be* sexy. I want to be... ravished. Shoved up onto a kitchen counter, because he just had to touch me and didn't care where it happened, as long as it did happen. I want no inhibitions and no time to think, just... do. I want the excitement of it all and the passion. I want, once and for all, to no longer care if people call me cute, because I have a guy who thinks I'm more, and I actually believe it.

"So, here goes.

"*Penis, dick, cock, peen, schlong, pecker, prick, shaft, weenie, willy, wanker, woody, chubby, boner, ding-a-ling, one-eyed-snake, kielbasa, knob, manhood, member, tent pole, trouser snake, tube steak, unit, wang, tally whacker, joystick, dong, dork, disco stick.*

"This is Heidi's Discount Erotica, over and out!"

Chapter 24

"ARE YOU SURE you want to do this?" I ask Brent tentatively. "Once we cross this line, there's no going back. This is serious business. This will change everything between us."

"I'm sure. I'm committed, and I'm not changing my mind. This is what I want, so move your hands and let me get in there."

With a sigh, I lift my hands from the mixing bowl on my kitchen counter as Brent starts scooping handfuls of things and dumping them in there.

"When I said you could put whatever you want in Nightmare Bars, it was kind of a joke," I tell him, grimacing when he dumps an entire jar of maraschino cherries on top of the crushed pretzels, broken up Hershey bars, shredded coconut, mini marshmallows, and crumbled potato chips.

"These are going to be amazing," he muses, picking up the wooden spoon and going to town on the mixture that now resembles vomit. Or something you'd find in a baby's diaper.

I'm momentarily distracted and can do nothing but mutter a low "Mmm" in response as I watch his biceps flex with each swirl of the spoon through the bowl. I have to grip tightly to the edge of the counter before I do something silly like wrap my hands around his muscles and say, *"Oooooh, you're so big and strong. I bet you could lift me up with no trouble at all!"*

When Brent suggested we spend the day doing something else "Minnesotan" so he could learn more about where he now lives, I told him he needed to learn how to bake bars. Cookie bars are a staple around here. We take them to birthdays, weddings, funerals, and everything in between. I'll admit my suggestion had ulterior motives. I pictured us getting in a flour fight, which would result in a lot of touching to get the flour off each other, then possibly some batter flinging, which would end in him licking it off me. Sadly, Brent is a very neat baker. He wipes down the counter after everything he touches and puts away canisters and ingredients as soon as he's finished using them. He even washed off the wooden spoon in between mixing the dry and wet ingredients.

"Tell me why they're called Nightmare Bars," he instructs as he continues to stir, and I try to think of a sexy way to dip my hand in the bowl and toss some batter in the general direction of my boobs.

I'm wearing too many clothes; that's the problem. I shouldn't have put an apron on over my dress. It's covering up the goods.

"When my uncle was little, he woke my grandma up from a nap to ask her what ingredients he needed to make her Seven Layer Bars," I explain as he dumps the lumpy mixture of questionable color on top of the graham cracker crust we already spread on the bottom of a pan. "She was half asleep and just rattled off a bunch of things and then told him to put whatever he wanted in there. So he did. And shockingly, they turned out delicious. My family started calling them Nightmare Bars, because there's no recipe; you just toss whatever you want in them, and they could turn out like a dream or they could be a complete nightmare."

When the mixture is spread out evenly on top of the crust, I put it in the oven and set the timer, untying my apron, pulling it over my head, and tossing it on the counter.

I still can't believe I'm standing in my kitchen, baking with a man. And not just any man, the man who I already know is quickly turning into a dream, and definitely not a nightmare. The last few weeks with him have been fun and easy, and it feels like we've known each other forever. It's nice being with a man I didn't grow up with, who doesn't already know everything about me, and without our families being lifelong friends. It's not embarrassing to bring up crazy stories about my childhood, like the time my dad took me ice fishing and I got so bored I stuck my tongue to a metal pole outside his fishing house to see if it would stick. If I told that story to another guy who grew up around here, he'd just roll his eyes and shake his head at me, because everyone around here knows that *of course* your tongue will stick to a metal pole in the middle of winter in Minnesota, and that's not funny at all. But Brent thought it was funny. He made me tell him every single detail of how I stood there with my tongue attached to a pole, trying to scream for my dad, who kept yelling back to me from inside the fish house, "Keep it down, Heidi! You'll scare all the fish away!"

"I need to ask you a question, and you have to promise not to make fun of me," Brent states as he finishes rinsing out the mixing bowl in my sink.

Is he going to ask me if he can touch my boobs? Oh, I hope he asks me if he can touch my boobs. Touch them! They're all yours!

When he turns around and leans against the sink as he dries off his hands, I decide to make it easy on him and move to stand right in front of him. With my hands on my hips and my chest pushed out, I know I look like a superhero getting ready for battle, but whatever works. Maybe he'll be so mesmerized by them he won't even ask and he'll just reach right out and grab them.

"I promise I won't make fun of you," I say.

"This is embarrassing," he mumbles, running one of his hands through his hair as he tosses the towel to the counter next to the sink.

My boobs are making him nervous. Oh, maybe this is why he hasn't made a move on me yet. He's got boob nerves! Nope. He's got tit nerves. Yeah, that's the good stuff. Tits.

"There's nothing to be embarrassed about. You know what—you don't even have to ask. Just go for it. Just reach right out and grab ahold of what you want," I suggest, taking a step closer so he doesn't even have to lean forward.

Boy, I should really get a gold star for being so helpful.

"Okay, I'm just gonna do it. I'm just gonna go for it," he says with a nod, pushing off the counter to stand up straight, the motion causing his chest to brush against mine.

Oh, that's nice. Do it! Do it already. Go for it!

"Heidi Larson, I don't want you dating anyone else but me," he blurts out.

"What the shit?" I mutter as my hands slowly drop from my hips.

He looks a little surprised that I just cursed, but I don't know how to take it back now. I thought he was going to make a move on me, and instead he's asking me to go steady. My boobs are sad, but it's the sweetest thing I've ever heard. He was nervous to ask me, and here I am standing in front of him with nothing but dirty thoughts on the brain. I need to fix this, fast.

"I mean, that's the shit!" I shout a little too loudly. "Oh jeez, I don't know why I can't stop saying *shit*."

Brent laughs, sliding his arms around my waist and pulling me against him. I wrap my arms around his shoulders and smile up at him, pushing up on my toes to give him a kiss.

"So, does that mean you want to go steady with me?" he asks with a wag of his eyebrows.

"Will I get to wear your class ring and letterman jacket and make all the girls in town jealous?"

"I have a hoodie that smells like me you can have. Will that work?"

Only if I can sleep in it with nothing on underneath, with you sleeping naked next to me, I think to myself.

"Oh, you betcha!" I chirp.

We stand here in my kitchen wrapped in each other's arms, and I think this is it. This is the moment when he'll just swipe everything off the counter and toss me up there. I won't even care if he breaks some stuff. Stuff can be replaced. This moment of counter sexy times cannot.

His hands grip tightly to the back of my dress like he's trying to hold himself back, and I want to scream at him that he doesn't need to hold back. I am fully on board for whatever dirty thought is on his mind.

The timer on my oven chooses that exact moment to go off, because of course it does.

"Nightmare Bars are done!" Brent cheers a little too excitedly, letting go of me and quickly scrambling over to the oven.

With a sigh of defeat, I watch him put on a pink, frilly oven mitt and remove the pan from the oven. After letting them cool for a few minutes, I cut them into squares and we each dig in. Surprisingly, Brent's

Nightmare Bar creation tastes much better than it looks, and we both eat half the pan before he looks at the clock hanging on the wall in my living room.

"I better go. I've got an early morning tomorrow for work. We're still on for dinner with your friends tomorrow night, right?"

I walk him to my door, trying to not let any disappointment show. It's fine. I'm not sad. He's a sweet man and he wants to take things slow. There's nothing wrong with that. Just because I've suddenly become sexually liberated doesn't mean we have to jump each other so soon. He doesn't want either one of us to date other people, he's making future plans with me that include meeting my friends, and he even mentioned wanting to meet my parents yesterday. He can bake, he cleans up after himself, he opens doors and pulls out chairs for me, he makes me laugh, he gets me all hot and bothered when we kiss, and he's sweet, and thoughtful, and kind. And who cares if he doesn't make any first moves? This is a good thing.

Brent gives me a kiss on the cheek, and I stand in the doorway, watching him walk over to his house, waiting to close the door until he's inside. Slumping my back against it, I tug my cell phone out of the pocket of my dress and pull up Aubrey's contact information, bringing it up to my ear as it rings, and I slide down the door onto my butt.

"I don't think Brent wants to have sex with me," I

say in greeting when she answers my call.

"Well, hello to you too. What do you mean he doesn't want to have sex with you? Didn't you tell me you guys have been making out like porn stars the last few weeks?"

I sigh, pulling my knees up to me and tugging the skirt of my dress over them.

"Okay, so, he probably, maybe wants to have sex with me. I've felt the evidence of his sexual desire a few times. I don't know. I think I'm just feeling sorry for myself. Why am I doing this? He's so perfect in every other way. I think I've read too many of those damn books lately. I want him to be like one of those alpha males. All growly and serious and breaking fine china just to have me."

Aubrey lets out her own sigh on the other end of the line as I let my head thump back against the door with the phone pressed to my ear.

"You need to remember, the guys I write about— and most authors write about—they're fictional, to an extent. We take what we know and we elaborate on it. We make it hotter. We make it more exciting. Life isn't perfect, and neither are relationships. People see my gorgeous, famous husband and then read my books and think, *'Wow, they clearly have non-stop sex that is always hot and their relationship must be flawless.'* I'm not going to write about how he farts in his sleep, and his idea of dirty talk is telling me it's okay to turn the sound off on the football game while we have a quickie on the couch. I write my books that way, because it's a fantasy. It's a way to escape, and dream, and imagine. Life is pretty boring if you don't have dreams, but you can't get so lost in the hoping and dreaming that you completely miss what's right in front of you," Aubrey explains. "You said so yourself; he's perfect. And you are one of the strongest women I've ever met. Don't let him not making a move on you ruin how far you've come. March your ass over to his house and ask him what the hell is up. *Communicate.* Say it with me, Heidi. Talk. To. Him."

She's right. She's absolutely right, and I'm an idiot. All these stupid signals I've been trying to send him and mentally screaming at him is childish. I'm a grown woman, and I need to be able to speak my mind, especially with the guy I'm dating, or this will never work.

"You're right. I'm gonna do it," I tell her, pushing up from the floor. "I'm going to go over there and just come right out and ask him if he wants me."

"That's my girl!" Aubrey cheers. "Go get 'em, tiger."

Ending the call, I toss the phone on the small side table by my front door, fling it open, and march across my yard, stomping up Brent's porch steps with determination. I bang my fist on the wood, giving myself a little pep talk as I wait for him to answer.

You can do this, Heidi. You have no problem telling thousands of strangers every intimate detail about your life. Brent isn't a stranger. You know him. You like him. And you want him to touch your butt. You just have to tell him to touch your damn butt already.

The door flies open when I'm still in the middle of my pep talk, throwing me a little off, but I quickly recover as Brent stands there in the doorway. He's got earbuds in his ears, attached to his cell phone that's in his hand, and his hair is sticking up all over the place like he was running his hands through it a million times. I feel a little bad that I interrupted whatever he was doing, but there's no time for sympathy now. I've got a butt that needs touching!

"Listen, Brent. I need to know if—"

All of a sudden, Brent grabs my hand and yanks me toward him, cutting me off as my body slams up against his. He jerks the earbuds out of his ears with one pull of the wire hanging down beneath his chin and then tosses everything to the side where I hear his phone land on the hardwood floor with a very loud *clunk* that doesn't sound very good.

Before I can get my bearings, one of his hands wraps around the back of my neck, his other arm bands around my waist, gripping me tightly to him, and his lips are crashing down against mine.

My mouth opens on a gasp of surprise, and he takes that opportunity to slide his tongue right in there and kiss me harder than he ever has before. There are sounds coming out of me I've never made in my life as he easily turns us, and my back is suddenly slamming into the wall behind me. I hear a picture frame rattle next to me on the wall, and I let out a squeak of shocked pleasure into his mouth.

It's not broken dishes, but a smashed phone screen is just as good.

His tongue is swirling around mine in the most amazing way, each swipe probing deeper and deeper until I'm gripping the front of his shirt so tightly in my fists I'm surprised it doesn't rip. Now I understand the meaning in romance books when a woman says she's drowning in a man's kiss. I feel like I can't catch my breath, and I will happily go under and die right now if this is how I go. Right when I think it can't possibly get any better than this, it happens.

Brent's touching my butt! Brent's touching my butt!

His hands grip my butt firmly, and he lifts me up against him, pressing me harder into the wall to anchor me in place. My legs wrap around his waist as he pushes himself between my thighs, and my arms fly around his shoulders to hold on tight.

B is for boner!

G is for grinding!

T is for tonguing! And thrusting! And oh my God, tits!

He completely devours me with his mouth while his hand comes up between our bodies and cups my breast in his palm, rubbing and massaging, while his hips are still swiveling and pushing between my legs, hitting just the right spot over and over again. My thighs tighten around his waist, and my hips respond to every move he makes, grinding and thrusting against him just as fast and hard. This moment is even better than anything I could have possibly imagined. Everything he's doing to me feels so good, and I never want it to end.

With each thrust of my hips, rubbing myself against Brent, I hear him let out a low growl in the back of his throat, and it's like a lit match to dynamite. Brent being the lit match, and the dynamite being my nether regions.

I can't believe this is what I've been missing out on all these years, dating nothing but complete duds. Oh, I'm so glad Brent isn't a dud! Brent is a dude! A hot, sweet, sexy dude with a growly alpha male lurking underneath all that sweetness.

Brent suddenly unwraps his hand from its hold on the back of my neck to smack his palm against the wall next to my head. His tongue starts plunging into my mouth with the same rhythm as the lower half of his body rubbing against me and…

Ohhh! Ohhh my! O is for orgasm! Sweet Lord almighty, O is for orgasm!

Maybe I should be embarrassed by how quickly the pleasure explodes out of me, but I'm not. No guy has ever successfully done this to me before, no matter how hard they fumbled around or awkwardly jerked against me, and this is *years* in the making, let me tell you. There is no fumbling and there is no awkwardness. Brent knows exactly what he's doing right now, and what he's doing is giving me an orgasm against the wall next to his front door. I'm moaning my pleasure so loudly into his mouth that I should actually be more embarrassed the neighbors might hear.

After a few more minutes of heavy kissing and small, remnant jerks of his hips between my legs, we both start slowing down until I loosen the death grip I have around his shoulders to press my hands to either side of his face. Both of his arms wrap loosely around me, his body now gently holding me in place against the wall instead of thrusting me up and down against it. Brent peppers a few more gentle kisses against my lips before slowly pulling his head back to look down at me, a sudden look of concern written all over his face.

"Are you okay? I didn't hurt you, did I?"

"If that's what you consider hurting, feel free to hurt me any time. Like, in about a half hour, after I recover. And then possibly an hour after that. Also, I'm free every day the rest of the week, including all day Saturday and Sunday."

Brent chuckles softly, reaching up to brush a strand of hair off my forehead that came loose from my ponytail, tucking it behind my ear.

"Not that I'm complaining or anything, but what was *that* for?" I ask softly, my body still vibrating and my skin still tingling.

He shrugs with a smirk. "I guess... Nightmare Bars just really, really excite me."

"Well, shit! I should have taught you how to make those things on our first date then!" I inform him, cutting off his laughter with a kiss.

Chapter 25

"**W**ELL, WHAT DO you guys think?"

Brent and I stand next to Jameson and Aubrey, no one saying a word as we stare straight ahead. When Brent expressed interest in wanting to meet my friends, I wasn't too certain Aubrey and Jameson would be up for it. They've pretty much kept a low profile since he's been in Minnesota, not really going out in public all that much. I figured bringing them to a small restaurant in Waconia would be as low profile as you could get, but he was still stopped and asked for pictures by several people when we were led through the restaurant to our table.

Jameson didn't seem to mind though, but that's probably because it's five-dollar burger night at Hopper's Bar and Grill, with all-you-can-eat tater tots. That will make anyone not care about pretty much anything.

It could also be because of Trevor, the hulking bodyguard who has stayed glued to their sides since Jameson and Aubrey met us here at the restaurant. He hasn't said one word to anyone, unless you count a few annoyed grunts as words, and he's had a permanent scowl on his face all night with his big, beefy arms crossed in front of him.

"I think it's tastefully inventive with a hint of whimsy, reminiscent of the Madrid-based artist, Irma Gruenholz. Looking at this sculpture is releasing endorphins that make me feel blissful," Trevor pipes up from behind us in a super deep, monotone voice that makes me jump when I hear it, and it does not sound at all blissful.

All four of us turn around and stare at Trevor with our mouths open.

"What? I like art. I'm gonna go talk to the owner about the fire exits."

With that, Trevor turns and exits the kitchen, needing to turn sideways to get his giant body to fit through the doorway.

"Seriously, you guys have nothing to say?" I ask after he's gone, shaking my head at all of them as we turn back around, because they aren't in awe right now.

Or maybe they are, and that's why no one is saying anything.

"It's a giant face. Made out of butter," Aubrey finally speaks up, cocking her head to the side to study the frozen butter sculpture sitting on a shelf in the walk-in freezer in the kitchen of Hopper's.

"It's not just any giant butter face; this is the Princess Kay of the Milky Way sculpture from 1981," I explain to them. "Donna Manning, the owner of Hopper's, was crowned Princess Kay at the state fair that year. Every Princess Kay gets her very own ninety-pound, exact replica of her face carved out of butter to do with as she wishes once the fair is over. One princess's family hosted a pancake breakfast for her entire town and let people scoop her face out for their breakfast. Another princess donated hers to her town's Corn Festival for their corn on the cob booth. Donna has kept hers in a freezer ever since, and she'll let anyone who asks come back and see it."

"That makes sense. I don't think I could eat my own face. That would just be weird," Aubrey states.

Jameson casually nudges me with his shoulder.

"Where's your Princess Kay of the Milky Way sculpture, Heidi?"

"Oh no, I don't have one of those! I've never been a Princess Kay. That would just be crazy." I laugh.

"Hey, your face would look amazing in butter," Jameson reassures me with a wink.

Brent quickly steps up and wraps his arm around my shoulders, pulling me against his side.

"Heidi's face is too beautiful. Butter could never do it justice."

Okay, this conversation is officially weird, even for me.

Brent has been doing things like this all night whenever Jameson says something to me or pays me any kind of attention. He'll find any opportunity he can to touch me, and one-ups any compliment Jameson might throw my way. When Aubrey and Jameson first walked into the restaurant and I gave Jameson a hug, as soon as I pulled away, Brent turned me around and kissed me, right in front of everyone. When we sat down at our table and Jameson told me the dress I was wearing was cute, Brent literally growled at him before kissing the side of my neck and whispering in my ear that my dress was *"hot as hell."* When Jameson laughed at something I said, Brent laughed even louder and put his hand on my thigh under the table. It's almost like he's...

Oh! Is Brent jealous of Jameson?

I've had a few beers tonight with dinner and my judgment could be off, and honestly, the fumes from a thirty-eight-year-old butter sculpture could be killing some of my brain cells right now, but I'm pretty sure Brent is doing whatever he can to remind Jameson that I'm with him. Which is just ridiculous. For every amount of attention Jameson has shown me, he's shown a thousand times more to Aubrey. *His wife.* They haven't been able to keep their hands off each other all night.

I should be completely appalled by his behavior, shouldn't I? I mean, I'm not his property. If another man wants to talk to me and throw me a compliment or two, it shouldn't make him act like a caveman who wants to smack me over the head with a log and drag me by my hair back to his cave.

And now I'm thinking about Brent pulling my hair. Clearly, I like the whole caveman routine. Who knew?

As Aubrey and Jameson walk away from the freezer and back through the kitchen, I grab Brent's hand and tug on it to stop him from following them. Walking right up to him, I push up on my toes, grab his face in my hands, and lay a hot and heavy kiss on him. A wolf-whistle from one of the kitchen workers forces us apart a few minutes later, both of us flushed and breathing heavy.

"What was that for?" Brent asks, rubbing his hands up and down my spine.

"I don't know. I guess... *butter sculptures* just really, really excite me," I tell him with a smile, pulling out of his arms, grabbing his hand, and leading him back out to the main part of the restaurant so we can finish our double date.

"JUST CLOSE YOUR eyes and relax!" I order, smacking my hands against Brent's chest, forcing him to fall backward and onto my couch.

I start giggling like a fool and then quickly apologize. "I'm sorry! Uff da, that was a little rough. I guess I like it rough! We're moving on to the rough stuff!"

It occurs to me that I probably shouldn't have had another glass of beer when we got back to our table at Hopper's. I'm not drunk, but I'm pleasantly buzzed, which makes me more word vomity than normal. I just want Brent to know that I appreciated his possessive jealousy. It was—I hate to say it, but I have to—*cute*. And sweet. This appreciation that's about to happen was the reason for that last glass of beer. Liquid courage and all.

"Just close your eyes and hold on tight, big boy," I tell him in my sultriest voice, quickly getting down on my knees on the floor, in between his legs. "Seriously. Close your eyes."

Once Brent has done as I've asked, I grab onto the button of his jeans with one hand while quickly reaching under the couch with my other hand, sliding out the book I shoved under there while he was in the bathroom.

Oh no! I lost the page I had it opened to!

Brent lifts his head up from the back of the couch when my hand just sits there like a useless slug on the crotch of his jeans, while I'm frantically trying to flip through the pages of the book down on the floor next to my knees with my other hand, trying my hardest to make sure the pages don't make any noise.

"No! Keep them closed! It will be more exciting that way!" I shout a little too forcefully, shoving against his chest again to get him to resume his previous position.

He still has an amused look on his face when he tilts his head back and closes his eyes, and I continue quietly flipping through the pages until the word **blowjob** catches my eye.

Eureka! I found it! Okay, let's get this party started. First step, blow gently on his penis. Wait. That can't be right. That can't be the first step. I haven't even taken his penis out yet! Where are the directions on how to take it out?

Biting my lip as I study the bulging crotch of his jeans, I just decide to go for it. With one hand reaching down and holding the place I need in the book, my other hand tugs on the button as hard as I can, forcing Brent's hips to jerk up off the couch. And the button to stay firmly hooked.

Did he superglue these stupid things on?

"Oopsie! Don't know my own strength!" I giggle nervously.

Making sure Brent's eyes are still closed, I quickly skim the chapter I'm holding open on the floor.

She spits into the palm of her hand before wrapping it around his hard cock... *Eeeeew, I have to spit on my hand to do this? That seems very unsanitary. Also, I still don't see the directions for taking it out! Why are we skipping steps here, people?*

Glancing up at Brent's face, he seems completely content to just sit there with his head back and his hands folded together on top of his stomach, letting me take the lead and do my thing. But I don't want him to be content. I want to drive him wild. And if driving him wild includes spitting on my hand, I guess I'm going to have to spit on my hand, dammit! I'll figure out how to get his thingy out afterward.

Bringing my palm up to my mouth, I bend my head forward and let as much saliva as I can drip down out of my mouth. And since I'm trying to be quiet, because I'm assuming the sound of me hacking into my own hand would not be sexy, the spit comes out in a long, stringy line that won't break free from my bottom lip.

Brent chooses that moment to pop his head back up, and I quickly slurp the spit back into my mouth in the most unladylike way, clamping my lips together tightly and giving him a big smile.

"What's going on down there?" Brent asks in amusement, leaning forward and resting his hands on my shoulders.

"Nothing! Nothing at all! Just getting all set up to put your... thingy in my mouth!" I inform him, smacking my hand down around on the floor, trying to blindly find the book and shove it back under the couch.

Brent leans to the side to see why my arm is flailing all around, bending down and scooping up the book, while I die a little of embarrassment. With his thumb holding it open where I had it, he flips it over.

Tie Me Up, Master!" Brent questions, reading the title out loud.

I knew I should have stuck with Aubrey's books and not chosen something out of my current reading level.

He flips the book back around and I watch as his eyes skim the page.

"Were you... about to spit in your hand?" he asks

tentatively, the corner of his mouth twitching.

"What? No! That's just crazy talk!" I laugh.

Brent sets the book down on the couch next to him, reaching up and swiping his thumb across my chin, right under my bottom lip.

"You had a little drool there," he says, barely able to contain his smile.

Dammit!

"Babe, you don't have to use an… erotic manual, so to speak, with me."

Oh, he should call me babe all the time. That was hot.

"But now that I've been getting in touch with my sensual side, I wanted to make sure I do it right and you enjoyed it, and there are so many confusing steps about this process. I thought you just stuck it in your mouth and went to town, and I really don't understand why they call it a blowjob, when you suck, you don't blow, unless you're doing that blowing air thing on it, which I still don't fully understand," I ramble. "It would be a cold breeze on your member. I thought that made them shrink? I feel like everything I know has been a lie."

I can't believe I just said "your member"! It's all fun and games being able to say "cock" on my podcast, but saying it in front of the guy I like is a whole other ballgame that will require more practice.

Brent chuckles softly before grabbing onto my sides, scooping me up from my knees, and swiftly placing me on his lap so I'm straddling his thighs.

So, this is how it's done! That wasn't hard at all.

"Listen to me, Heidi," Brent says softly, cupping my face in his hands and forcing me to look at him. "We don't have to do anything you're not comfortable with or ready for."

"I'm comfortable and I'm ready, I swear! Are we moving too fast? Is this too much for you?"

"Nothing you do is ever too much for me. I will move at whatever speed you want. Fast, slow, supersonic, or grandma in the middle of traffic with a walker."

I sigh at his sweet words, licking my lips and swallowing quickly before I start talking again.

"I like the speed we're going. I would not mind one bit moving faster and mowing down that grandma in her walker. I want to experience everything with you, because I trust you. I'm just... nervous. I'm afraid I won't do it right, or you won't like what I do, or it won't turn you on, and I thought if I did exactly like it said in that book, it would be perfect," I explain. "But they skipped the part about taking it out of your pants, and I'm confused on how that works without catching it on your zipper. Was I supposed to pull your pants off? You still have your shoes on. Was I supposed to take those off as well? Why didn't they say that? They just skipped right to the spitting!"

He rubs his thumbs gently back and forth against my cheeks, making my limbs feel all melty and gooey, even when I'm having a slight sexual breakdown.

"I will like anything you and I do together, no matter what it is; I guarantee it. Because I like *you*. I like everything about you. You turn me on just by being in the same room with me. It was also pretty hot to hear you say the word *blowjob,* and *suck,* and if we're being honest, *member* kind of did it for me too." He shrugs. "I don't ever want you to feel nervous with me. We can stop until you're more comfortable. We don't have to do anything right now. We can watch a movie or something."

"No! We're not stopping. I just… need to get over my nerves. Quick! Tell me the most embarrassing thing that ever happened to you."

Lifting myself up on my knees a little, I scoot forward, resting my hands on his shoulders before pushing my body back down more snugly against his lap and moving around a little to get comfortable, my eyes widening in surprise.

Oh my, he wasn't kidding. I really do turn him on just by being in the same room with him. Obviously, because what just happened in the last few minutes was definitely not hot.

"Sorry, I have no control over my dick when you're sitting on my lap, wiggling your cute little ass around like that," he informs me, resting his hands on my hips to stop me from moving. "Most embarrassing story, huh?"

I nod quickly, almost wanting to tell him to forget it. When he put me on his lap and I got myself situated, the skirt of my dress rode up, and right now, the hardness in his pants is pressed right up against me, with nothing separating us but my flimsy scrap of underwear and the rough material of his jeans that is doing some amazing things down there.

"My mom once walked in on me masturbating," he says easily.

"Oh no! That couldn't have been fun. But, I mean, boys do that sort of thing all the time when they're teenagers, I've heard, so don't be embarrassed about that," I reassure him.

"It was three months ago," he deadpans, which makes me throw my head back and laugh.

"No!"

"Yes." He nods once I've gotten myself under control and just a few small giggles are still coming out.

"In my defense, it was *your* fault."

"What? How was it *my* fault?"

"I was looking out my front window, and you were outside doing some gardening in a tank top and a pair of ratty jean shorts, and you bent over, and... yeah."

My gardening outfit turned him on? This just keeps getting hotter and hotter, and I am kicking myself for not making a move on him sooner.

"So, anyway," he continues, his hands moving off my hips to rest on top of my bare thighs. "When you move across the country and get your own place, you assume you have all the privacy in the world. Until your dick is in your hand and you suddenly remember you gave your mother a spare key the last time you went to visit her. And she showed up out of the blue to surprise me. I don't think either one of us could have been more shocked when she walked through my front door."

We both laugh softly when he finishes with his story, and now his palms are skimming gently up and down my thighs, inching a little bit higher under my dress each time he glides them back up.

"I think my nerves are gone now," I whisper, shifting myself on his lap and pressing my forehead against his.

He lets out a low groan, his hands moving the rest of the way up under my skirt until they're gripping my hips, slowly helping my lower body rock against him.

"Are you sure?" he whispers back.

With confidence I didn't think I possessed a few minutes ago, I remove one hand from his shoulder and slide my hand down his chest, lifting myself up a little, my fingers easily unsnapping and unzipping his jeans now that I'm not thinking so hard about it. I let my hand slide right inside his pants and wrap it around him, which makes him let out an even louder groan.

"We need to move somewhere else. You deserve... better than... sex on a couch," he stutters as I start moving my hand up and down around his length between my thighs.

"I've only ever had sex on a bed. And one time in the back of a car, and that was horrible and I never want to repeat it again," I speak softly, squeezing harder and moving my hand faster, smiling to myself as I listen to him pant against my mouth. "I've never had couch sex. I want to have couch sex with you, and I think we can—"

He cuts me off with his mouth, quickly reaching between us and removing my hand from around him. As he kisses me, I'm happy to find out he's much better at the one-handed thing than I am. With one of his hands now firmly clutching my butt under my dress, he shifts his hips up, and uses his other hand to pull his wallet out of his back pocket, fumbling around next to us on the couch until I hear the crinkle of a foil wrapper.

Breaking the kiss, I look down between us and watch him pull himself out of his jeans. Without taking my eyes off of what he's doing, I quickly scramble off his lap, reach up under my dress, and slide my underwear down, flinging it somewhere across the room as he sheathes himself with a condom.

"Jesus, you're so hot," Brent mumbles as he stares up at me standing before him.

My lips feel swollen from his kisses, my face feels flushed in anticipation, my chest is heaving, my dress is a wrinkled mess, I'm standing between his spread knees not wearing any underwear, and I've never felt sexier or more wanted in my life.

Faster than I've ever moved before, I climb back on his lap, lifting my skirt up to my upper thighs as I straddle him again. Brent leans up and meets me halfway, attacking my mouth again with another hot kiss that drives me crazy, and makes me start rubbing myself against him, eager to keep going and share this with him.

I let out a little whimper when he pulls his lips away from mine, his hands framing my face as he looks at me.

"You're sure you're sure?" he asks again.

His need to be absolutely certain I'm okay with this makes something inside me *pop*, and I wonder if this is what it feels like to fall head-over-heels for someone.

"I'm sure I'm sure," I tell him.

"Take what you want, Heidi. I'm all yours."

Pressing my lips back to his, I reach down between us again, wrap my hand around him, and guide him between my legs. As I sink down on top of him, we groan in unison, and I'm pretty sure my eyes roll into the back of my head.

We never stop kissing once as I cling to his shoulders, and he keeps his arms locked securely around me as I slowly start moving up and down on top of him. I never worry once if I'm doing it right or if it's good for him. I can tell by the way he thrusts his hips up to meet me, wanting more. I can tell with each of his moans of pleasure that I swallow with every kiss, and I can tell by how tight his arms get around me when I push my body down, taking him as deep as he'll go while grinding against him that he's right here with me, enjoying each and every dirty moment of having sex on my couch.

I do exactly as he says, and I take what I want.

And it is the best. Moment. Ever.

Chapter 26

Heidi's Discount Erotica, Episode 9

"**W**ELCOME TO HEIDI'S Discount Erotica, do-do-do! I just want to start off this podcast with a great big thank you to all my listeners. I began this thing on accident, because I was lost and frustrated with my life, and it turned into an outlet for me to talk about my frustrations and fix what I thought was broken inside myself. Through all your supportive comments, and with a little help from my sexy neighbor, I've come to realize there was nothing broken within me. There were just a few wires crossed between my brain and my soul. I didn't need to change everything about who I am as a person to get what I wanted. I'm always going to be a little dorky, and a little weird, and that's okay! I just needed to believe in myself. To believe that I'm more than the labels I've given myself and that I've allowed other people to give me. I needed to believe that I can be dorky and weird, and still be confident and sexy. I think I've learned through all this that I had those qualities inside me all along; I just needed to figure out how to channel them. So thank you for listening to me ramble week after week. Thank you for giving me an outlet to learn how to believe in myself, one messy, dorky step at a time.

"Okay, onto the good stuff! I'm happy to report that things with my sexy neighbor have been... sexy. Oh so sexy. Every minute I spend with him is better than the last, because he lets me be who I am. He doesn't judge me. He doesn't make fun of me if I stumble. I've learned that the sexiest thing about a man isn't necessarily how he looks with his clothes off—although it's a definite perk when he works in construction and has muscles for days. And it's not how he knows exactly the right way to touch you to make you scream like a wild woman—but you know, that's also a bonus. The sexiest thing about a man is when he has confidence in the woman he's with. When he believes in her, and encourages her, and supports her, no matter what crazy ideas go through her head.

"Which brings us to today's excerpt—a crazy idea that's been going through my head for the last week and a half since we first... you know, christened our relationship. And my couch. And have since christened my kitchen counter, his bed, my living room floor, his shower, and one amazing evening in my backyard, on a blanket under the stars, next to a fire in the new fire pit he built for me. I want to try something new and bold with him. So, I'm just going to read a little something to give me a few pointers and get the juices flowing!

"Oh. Eeew. Maybe I shouldn't say juices. That word never seemed gross to me before, but now that my head is full of dirty things, it's not good. Not good at all. Moving on! For all you Penelope Sharp fans, I asked her to write me a little something to help me out with this, and she delivered! Here we go.

"*Alexis had never felt so much power with a man before. As she finished tying Drake's wrists to the bedposts, she took a moment to stand next to the bed, admiring her work.*

His muscular biceps flexed as he tested the restraints, staring at her with fire in his eyes, waiting for her to make the next move. Her eyes trailed down his bare chest and stomach to stop on his hard cock, resting heavily on his stomach, twitching with desire when she licked her lips as her eyes took their fill.

He lay before her like an erotic buffet, and she didn't know what she should sample first. She wanted to taste every bit of this delicious meal, all at once. Climbing onto the bed and straddling his thighs, she didn't waste one minute. She wanted to drive him wild. She wanted to hear the bedposts rattle and creak as he strained against the silk ties. Wrapping her hand around his thick erection, she started pumping it slowly up and down. When Drake moaned and his eyes started to flutter closed, she quickly removed her hand, which forced him to let out a frustrated growl.

'Keep your eyes open and watch what I'm doing to you,' she ordered.

Drake immediately complied. As a reward, when she wrapped her hand around him again, Alexis leaned her body forward and took the entire length of his cock in her mouth. She sucked harder and harder on him with each bob of her head up and down his shaft, and within seconds, she got exactly what she wanted.

Alexis heard the rattle and creak of the bedposts as Drake strained against them, muttering curses into the otherwise quiet room as she brought him to ecstasy, swallowing every last drop as it poured down her throat.'"

"Oh jeez, does anyone else need a cigarette right now? My goodness. This is Heidi's Discount Erotica, signing off. I've got a sexy neighbor to tie to my bedposts, don'tcha know!"

Chapter 27

"**H**EIDI... OH, JESUS...." Brent mutters in a broken voice as I go to town on his penis like I've been doing this sort of thing all my life.

I'd smile in victory that he seems to really like what I'm doing, going by the noises he's making, but it's really hard to smile when you have a penis in your mouth and you're trying to concentrate. There's just so much to remember. Lick, suck, don't squeeze too hard, don't squeeze too soft, keep your head and your hand moving at the same time, don't gag or drool too much...

Wait. I think it's okay if I gag and drool. I think I read guys like that.

I make the mistake of gagging *on* my drool, and a very unsexy sound comes out of my mouth.

"Are you okay?" Brent suddenly asks with concern in his voice, his head popping up from the pillow and his arms tugging against the restraints.

Keeping my mouth on him, I remove my hand and give Brent a quick thumbs-up before going back to work, the sounds that are coming out of him making me feel like a goddess and totally turning me on.

I borrowed two of my dad's silk ties when I went over to my parents' house for dinner the other night, and I'm so glad Aubrey wrote about that in her excerpt. I was just planning on using some spare rope I had in the trunk of my car, or maybe some zip-ties I have in the junk drawer in my kitchen. These silk ties seem much more comfortable than the rope. And not as murdery as the zip-ties. And the pretty paisley patterns are very fun and festive.

Removing my mouth from Brent's impressive erection that is all thanks to me and my "tie him up and drive him wild" idea, I climb up his naked body and straddle him, leaning forward to rest my hands on either side of his head on the bed.

"Do you like this? Is it okay?" I whisper, bending down and kissing his cheek before trailing kisses down to the side of his neck.

"This is more than okay. But I hate not being able to touch you," he moans when I use my teeth to nip gently at the skin of his neck. "And you're wearing too many clothes."

When I first told him about my idea, he didn't even hesitate or question me. He grabbed the ties that I held up in front of him then grabbed my hand and pulled me back to my bedroom. He even happily complied with my softly spoken order of, "Strip. And lay down on the bed." He is such a team player. I was so busy making sure the ties were secure and giving him pleasure that I didn't even think about taking my own clothes off. I can't even believe how erotic it is to be straddling him right now, when he's in the buff and I'm still wearing the pale blue LuLaRoe dress I wore to church this morning.

Is it wrong to be doing this sort of thing on the Lord's day? I really hope not.

As I continue licking and sucking on the side of his neck, I grind myself down on top of him. I'm rewarded with the sound of him jerking roughly against the restraints, while his hips thrust up to meet me.

Pushing myself away from him, I sit up fully on top of his body, trailing my fingertips down his beautifully sculpted chest, across his stomach that he sucks in with a sharp breath when I skim my fingernails across it gently, before grabbing the hem of my dress that's lying in a pool all around him. He watches me with hooded eyes as I slowly start to lift it up, baring my thighs, my white lacy underwear, and my stomach, before pausing.

Brent jerks his arms, and the bedframe rattles against the wall behind it as he lets out a frustrated growl.

"Fuck You are so hot. I need to touch you," he pleads, his eyes staring right between my thighs and driving me crazy, making me rock against him.

I continue slowly lifting the hem of my dress, more and more of my body coming on display, until suddenly, my worst nightmare comes to life.

"Heidi! Yoo-hoo! Are you home?"

My eyes widen in shock, Brent's face mirroring mine.

"Who the hell is that?" he asks in a panic as I clamber off his lap and start running around the room like a chicken with its head cut off.

"Oh, it's fine! It's just my mom!"

His face gets white as a sheet, and I wince that our perfect afternoon of some friendly bondage has gone to crap. Now the sounds of Brent tugging against the silk ties is no longer one of want and need just for me, and it's all about sheer terror.

"Heidi! I brought my toolbox to fix that leak under your kitchen sink!" my dad shouts from what sounds like the entrance to my hallway that leads right back here.

"And my dad," I add sheepishly as I race around the room, scooping up his jeans, and his t-shirt, and his socks, and his boxer briefs, while poor Brent continues to curse and yank on his arms, the lower half of his body thrashing around back and forth on my bed.

"Heidi? Are you in here?" my mom shouts, her voice right outside the door.

Brent starts struggling against the restraints in earnest now. He's tugging and still muttering curses under his breath, with beads of sweat pebbling on his forehead, while I continue running around in circles at the foot of the bed like an idiot, just hugging his clothes to my chest.

"Untie me! For the love of God, untie me!" he orders in a loud, freaked-out whisper.

I hear the sound of my bedroom doorknob being

turned, and there's no way I can untie him in time, and we both know it.

I used double knots, for God's sake! Do you have any idea how hard it is to untie a double-knotted silk tie? I don't actually know, but going by how hard he was pulling on them when I had his penis in my mouth, and how red and angry his hands look right now as he continues jerking on them, I'm pretty sure I might have to cut those things off him.

With seconds to spare, I do what any rational woman would do in this situation. I toss his clothes to the side, yank the pillow out from under his head, and plop it right down on top of his junk, before turning around to face the door with a big smile on my face.

"There you are!" my mom says brightly as she swings the door open. "Why didn't you answer me when—"

Her words cut off as soon as she looks beyond me, her mouth dropping open in shock.

"Uff da, you can't just stop in the doorway like that, Peggy," my dad complains as he gently pushes her shocked, frozen body out of the way and enters the room, immediately stopping in his tracks.

"Oh, hey there, Mom and Dad! How's it going? What are you guys up to today? Just out for a Sunday afternoon drive? It's beautiful outside. We were just talking about going to the Minnesota Landscape Arboretum to check out the botanical gardens," I ramble.

"Who needs the botanical gardens when you've got a

fern right here?" my mom mutters, her eyes never leaving Brent.

"What's going on here, Heidi? Is this a burglar or something? Are you in danger? Where's your cell phone. I'll call the police," my dad states, starting to back out of the room.

My mom quickly reaches out and grabs his arm to stop him.

"Henry, remember that thing we talked about doing last week from that book I read, and you said no because you already have bad circulation in your hands?"

My dad silently looks back and forth between me and Brent for a few seconds. I see the lightbulb go on in his head when his eyes get as big as saucers, before quickly giving Brent a dirty look with narrowed eyes and a curl of his upper lip.

Brent clears his throat behind me.

"Mr. and Mrs. Larson, it's lovely to finally meet you. I'm Brent Miller, your daughter's neighbor and boyfriend. Heidi's told me so much about you," Brent says in an overly cheerful voice.

I turn around and give him a grateful smile. The poor, poor man is meeting my parents for the first time in the buff, tied to my bed. A lesser man would probably be crying and would denounce any kind of boyfriend status just to save himself from imminent death by humiliation, but Brent is clearly not a lesser man. He's the *best* man.

"Are those my ties?" my dad suddenly asks.

Oh no.

"My funeral ties? Heidi Marie Larson, did you use my funeral ties for... this?"

"I fixed the leak under Heidi's kitchen sink!" Brent shouts quickly to try to get my dad to stop glaring at his funeral ties.

"Well, aren't you just a sweetheart!" Mom praises. "Henry, isn't he just a sweetheart?"

My dad doesn't answer. He just continues giving Brent the evil eye from over by the door.

"Dad, Brent's in construction. He's very good with his hands!"

I realize the error of my words when my mom immediately giggles.

"Oh, sure, when they aren't tied up," she states through her laughter. "That can't be comfortable. Heidi, untie the poor man."

"The knots are a little... tight at the moment. I don't think I can get them undone," I tell her in a quiet voice, my face heating with embarrassment.

"Let me see if I can get them. I'm good with knots."

"*No!*" Brent and I both shout at the same time when she starts moving toward the bed.

"I mean, no thank you, ma'am. That's very kind of you to offer, but I'm fine. I can't feel my fingers anymore, but it's fine! I'm good," Brent reassures her.

"She's had a loose step on her front porch. I noticed

that was fixed on my way in. Was that you as well?" my dad asks Brent, crossing his arms in front of him.

"Yes, sir, I fixed that step a few weeks ago," Brent confirms, lifting his head and nodding between his arms strung up above him.

"What about the jiggling toilet handle in her guest bathroom?"

"Fixed that too," Brent says with a smile. "Along with the window that wouldn't open in the spare bedroom, and the wobbly dining room table leg."

Silence fills the room as my dad continues staring Brent down, and my armpits start sweating so badly I'm afraid my dress will forever be ruined by pit stains.

After a few tense minutes, my dad finally drops his arms to his sides and lets out a sigh.

"I'll go outside and get my hedge trimmers from the trunk to cut the boy loose," my dad finally speaks as he turns away from us, shouting once he's back out in the hall. "But for God's sake, put some pants on him before I get back!"

"I'll just go start heating up the chicken and broccoli hotdish I brought over for lunch. Brent, you're going to love my chicken and broccoli hotdish. It's one of Heidi's favorites," Mom tells him happily before also exiting the room.

Once we're alone again, I turn and crawl up onto the bed next to Brent, giving him a quick kiss of apology before resting my forehead against his.

"I really think that went well." Brent nods against me. "But maybe when we're telling this story to our future grandchildren, we could leave the whole naked bondage thing out it."

Oh, why did he have to go and say something like that? Now I have no choice in the matter. I am one hundred percent in love with him.

Chapter 28

*I*F YOU WOULD have told me a few months ago that I'd have a serious boyfriend, and it would be so natural and easy being with him, and I'd be the happiest I'd ever been in my life and making plans for the future, I would have laughed in your face. Politely, of course, because that's the Minnesota way.

My limited experiences with boyfriends were definitely nothing serious, and there was not one thing natural or easy about being with them. I was constantly on edge, watching what I said and what I did, so I wouldn't scare them away with my weirdness. And I was never really sad when we ultimately ended. There were no tears. There were no fights. There weren't even really break-ups. We'd go out to dinner or something, and then, I'd just never hear from him again until we ran into each other at church or some other town function. We'd make polite conversation, and it was like we'd never had our tongues in each other's mouths or seen each other naked.

As cliché as it sounds, being with Brent is as easy as

breathing. When we disagree about something, I'm not filled with anxiety that this is it. This is when he'll realize I'm too much. He accepts me for who I am, which means I'm never afraid to *be* who I am. I can be awkward and trip over my own two feet, or I can be sexy and take control. I can ramble a bunch of crazy nonsense, or I can have a passionate conversation about something I believe in. We can have sweet, normal sexy times where we cuddle and watch television afterward, or I can tie him to my bedposts and my parents walk in on us, followed by a chicken and broccoli hotdish lunch where no one mentions that my dad had to cut him loose with his hedge clippers, and the two of them just spend the hour arguing about football. Although, it's been three weeks and Brent still shudders when he sees a tie.

Brent never judges me, he never makes fun of me, and he never rolls his eyes at me when I'm being ridiculous, like when we had a twenty-minute argument the other day about how Jell-O salad is absolutely considered a salad, and anyone who thinks otherwise is wrong. Sadly, that argument ended in a draw, because he wouldn't back down, going on and on about his fancy L.A., disgusting kale nonsense, but it's fine. We made up by getting naked. Brent just lets me be *me*, no matter which *me* decides to come out at any given time.

"You look good wearing my sweatshirt," Brent says from his bed, with a lazy smile on his face.

He's lounging against the pillows with his hands

folded behind his head, watching me pick up my clothes that are strewn all over his floor. I'm wearing nothing but one of his oversized sweatshirts I stole from his closet. It has his construction company name on it and hangs down to the middle of my thighs.

"I'm running out of clothes to wear. I need to do some laundry today," I tell him, tossing a few of his dirty clothes into the pile I'm making at the end of his bed without even thinking about it.

Our dirty clothes are comingling. This is definitely serious.

One of the best things about living next door to your boyfriend is, I've never packed a bag when I've spent the night here. It started off that way, because I never wanted to just assume he'd *want* me to sleep over. And now, it's just easier for one of us to walk over to my house and grab whatever else I might need.

"Babe, you don't have to do my laundry."

Gaaah! There's the "babe" thing again. I'll never get tired of hearing him say that.

"I don't mind! I have to do mine anyway. And besides, you've cooked dinner for us every night this week," I remind him.

That's another amazing thing about Brent that I thought only happened in books. He actually knows how to cook, and he's pretty good at it. *And* he does the dishes. Someone needs to pinch me. It's like I'm living my very own fairytale romance.

I should tell him I love him. Crap! I should tell him about my podcast first, shouldn't I? I'm standing here thinking about all the ways he's perfect, and I'm being a wuss for no reason. Well, aside from the whole creepy stalker reason.

"Listen, I need to tell you—"

"Oh! Hold that thought," Brent interrupts me, flinging the blankets off his body. "I forgot I have a present for you."

I definitely hold that thought and let a bunch of dirty thoughts take over when he so casually gets out of bed completely naked, walking over to his dresser and grabbing a pair of sweatpants from his bottom drawer. I lick my lips as I watch him pull them on, knowing I'll never be able to concentrate on anything else that comes out of his mouth after this point. It's bad enough those sweatpants are hanging low on his hips and I can see every inch of his glorious chest and those delicious indents down by his hips, but I'm also fully aware he's not wearing any underwear under those sweatpants. He's just hanging loose in there, and goodness, why is that such a turn on?

I'm still standing at the foot of his bed, thinking about all the dirty things I'd like to do to him, when he returns a few minutes later with a large box in his hands and gives it to me.

"What's this?" I ask in surprise as I turn and sit down on the edge of the bed, setting the box on my bare thighs.

"Just something I wanted to get you. It took a while

for me to find the exact one, but… just open it," Brent orders excitedly, a huge smile on his face that I want to kiss, because he looks like a little boy on Christmas morning right now.

His blue eyes are sparkling, and he's practically bouncing up and down as he stands right in front of me. I can't help but laugh at his eagerness as he rubs his hands together when I start to pull the packing tape off the top of the box to get it open. As soon as I lift the flaps and pull out the bubble wrap, I see something nestled inside, wrapped in white tissue paper.

"Careful. It's breakable," he warns seriously as I pull it out, which just makes me laugh again.

When I gently unwrap the tissue paper, my amused smile is replaced with a gasp of surprise when I finally see what he got me.

It's a teal, Red Wing pottery vase. But not just *any* teal, Red Wing pottery vase. It's the exact same one that my grandmother gave me that I smashed into a hundred pieces not that long ago.

"Oh my gosh. My grandmother's vase," I whisper, turning it around in my hand and running my fingertips over it in awe. "I can't believe you found this."

My eyes fill with happy tears that he did something so thoughtful. This vase isn't worth a lot of money, but it was sentimental to me, because it was my grandmother's. I have no idea how he was able to find the exact same one, but he did. I don't even remember telling him about breaking that vase and how sad I was about it. I'm pretty sure I only mentioned it on

Oh my God! Oh no.

My heart starts trying to beat its way out of my chest, and my hands are shaking so badly I have to put the vase back inside the box and set it down on the bed next to me before I drop it. I quickly go back over every conversation we've ever had, knowing without a shadow of a doubt that I never told him about that vase. And yet he knew about it. And there's only one way he *could* have known.

Oh, God. I think I'm going to be sick.

Looking up at him slowly, confusion is written all over his face that I've suddenly become quiet and not at all as happy as I was moments ago. I'm sure I look like someone just murdered one of my family members. I *feel* like someone just murdered one of my family members.

"I never told you about breaking that vase," I whisper as a tear escapes from my eye and trails down my cheek.

I thought it was a good thing that I've come to know Brent so well and can tell everything he's thinking just by looking at his face. But watching his Adam's apple bob as he swallows nervously, and *knowing* he's suddenly panicking, does not make me feel good at all.

"Sure you did," he replies, nodding quickly. "It was on your coffee table and you kicked it over and…."

He trails off, and I get to experience the misery of

watching his face quickly morph from panic to sadness that he suddenly realizes the error he made by giving me this vase. Or maybe it's pity I'm seeing on his face. Who's to know at this point? Now, I don't even know what the hell I'm looking at on his face. I'm embarrassed, and I'm sad, and I'm so damn confused.

"You know. You listened. You listened and you never said anything?" I whisper brokenly, swiping angrily at the tears falling down my cheeks as I stand up from the end of the bed and move away from him.

"Heidi," Brent says softly, reaching out and grabbing my arm as I pass him.

I jerk my arm out of his hold and continue walking until I'm over by the door and there's enough space between us so I can think clearly.

"Did you just listen to that one? Or did you listen to all of them?"

It would be bad enough if he just listened to that one. Episode five, where I read an excerpt about oral sex and had to drink wine just to get the nerve to ask him out on a date.

When he closes his eyes and lets out a defeated sigh, running one of his hands nervously through his hair before he looks at me again, I have my answer. For a split second, I was still holding onto hope that maybe he'd chuckle and ask me what the hell I was talking about and give me some kind of plausible explanation, like maybe I talked about it in my sleep one night or something. I know that's not really a plausible explanation, but it would make me feel a lot better than what's actually happening.

"All of them," he whispers guiltily.

Brent listened to Heidi's Discount Erotica, and he knows... everything. Every mortifying, embarrassing thing.

I can physically feel my heart snapping in two and breaking into more pieces than my grandmother's vase.

"It was an accident. I swear to you, Heidi," he explains quickly, taking a step toward me, which makes me take a step back until I bump into his bedroom wall behind me. "I listen to this podcast called Herb's Discount Building, and it's all about remodeling on a budget, and one night, I did a search for it to listen to the newest episode, and your podcast must have come up in the search. I clicked on it without paying attention. Suddenly, I heard this voice that I recognized, and then when you said your name, I knew it was you. I know I should have turned it off when you started talking about me, but I couldn't help it. You were just so sweet, and adorable, and I felt bad that—"

"Stop!" I shout, tears of humiliation falling fast and hard down my face. "You don't get to call me sweet and adorable anymore. You've been listening this entire time? To everything? Oh my God, you must think I'm so pathetic. Is that why you said yes to that first date? Because you felt *sorry* for me? Your poor, dorky neighbor who couldn't talk to a man she liked without giggling and looking like a fool. The pitiful woman who lives next door and has to read from erotic books just to get some confidence and learn how to be sexy. Boy, this must have been a nightmare for you, pretending like you actually gave a shit about someone so childish and ridiculous."

Since I made the mistake of blocking myself in when I backed into the wall, I have nowhere to go when Brent charges across the room and cups my face in his hands.

"I never, *never* thought any of those things about you, Heidi. You have to believe me. Everything between us is real. Everything I feel about you is real. I didn't go out with you because I pitied you. I went out with you, because I *wanted* to. Because I've wanted to since the first moment I met you, when you knocked on my door and welcomed me to the neighborhood with a chicken casserole," he tries to explain, swiping my tears away with his thumbs.

I don't even care about arguing with him that it's called a hotdish and not a casserole. I don't care about anything aside from wishing a hole would open in the floor and swallow me up. I've never been so embarrassed in my life. I fully planned on poking a little fun at myself when I finally came clean and told him about the podcast, and I pictured us having a good laugh about it, because I would be in control of the situation. And let's be honest, those podcasts *are* a little silly. But this... knowing he's been listening to me this entire time and never said a word... knowing he's heard my deepest, darkest insecurities without my knowledge and used them to his advantage for whatever reason, it hurts. It hurts so badly I can't breathe. Regardless of how silly those podcasts were, they were *mine*. And I was proud of them and all the ways they helped me break out of my shell. Now, I'm just ashamed of them. I'm disgusted with myself that I couldn't just be a normal woman, with a normal crush, who could have a normal relationship without needing help.

"You were so shy, and sweet, and your smile lit up my world," Brent continues, my face still held in his hands, because I just don't have the energy to move away. "Growing up in L.A., I spent my entire life surrounded by vapid women who intimidated me and made me feel like I wasn't good enough. That my looks weren't good enough, that my career wasn't good enough, that my family wasn't rich enough, that the car I drove and the house I lived in weren't fancy enough. You never made me feel that way. You made me like myself and the choices I made with my life. You made me want to do everything I could to be a good person so you'd want to be with me. I shouldn't have listened to your podcast without telling you, and I'm so sorry I did. But I also wouldn't have known how you felt about me if I hadn't. I didn't think you gave two shits about me, which is why *I* never asked *you* out."

God, I want to believe him, but how can I? Every

word he says should be lighting me up inside, but it just feels like he's stabbing a knife right into my heart. The more I go over everything I said and did in those podcasts, the more I start to question *everything* about our relationship. When I get to one particular episode in my head, a painful gasp flies out of my mouth and I finally find the energy to wrench out of his hold on my face and move away from him to stand in the doorway.

"That night I came over to your house because I was frustrated with weeks and weeks of always making the first move, and you yanked me inside and gave me an orgasm against your wall, you were wearing earbuds." The realization of what happened that night is making me feel sicker and sicker until I have to press my hand to my stomach to keep going. "I *just* got done uploading a podcast about how I wanted you to take charge and be all alpha male after you left my house, and like some magical fucking unicorn, you did exactly what I wanted. God, I thought you were so perfect, just seeming to *know* what I wanted without me having to say anything, but you were listening. Oh my God, you were listening! Do you have *any* idea how mortifying that is?"

I'm practically choking on my tears at this point, and my hand moves from my stomach to clamp tightly over my mouth before I start wailing. Turning away from him, I quickly make my way out of his room and down the hall, not even caring that I'm leaving all my clothes behind and I'm only wearing his sweatshirt. I need to get out of here. I need to get away from him before I make any more of a fool of myself with all the tears and the snot that just won't stop.

"Heidi, please! Don't go!" Brent shouts, his bare feet pounding on the hardwood floor as he races after me.

As soon as my hand wraps around the handle of his front door, I feel him against my back, reaching over my shoulder and pressing his palm against the wood to stop me from opening it. My head drops forward, and I squeeze my eyes closed when his free arm wraps around my waist and he holds me securely against the front of him.

"I'm sorry," he whispers, his mouth pressed right against my ear. "I'm so fucking sorry. I should have told you, but I couldn't. I didn't want to ruin anything about what you were doing. I was so proud of you, watching you come out of your shell and doing it all on your own; you have no idea. You amaze me, and I'm so goddamn proud of you. Please, believe me. I never meant to hurt you. I never meant to make you feel embarrassed. I love you. I love everything about you, and I can't lose you, Heidi."

Everything I always wanted to hear, not just from any man, but from this man, and it doesn't matter.

"That's where you're wrong," I whisper, opening my eyes and lifting my chin to stare blindly at the door in front of me. "I *didn't* do it all on my own, did I? You listened to everything. You knew what I wanted, and you made sure it happened. It's like every woman's fantasy come to life. A guy who can read her mind and give her what she wants. But you didn't read my mind. You fucking listened to every word of it without telling me, and you used it to your advantage."

"Heidi—"

I cut him off by shoving my shoulders back against his chest to push him away from me, yanking open the door when his hand drops from it. I walk right out into the early morning sunshine wearing nothing but his stupid sweatshirt and a face full of tears and humiliation as my fairytale turns into one giant lie and crumbles all around me.

Chapter 29

"**W**HAT IS THAT god-awful smell?"

I don't even bother lifting my head from my parents' couch. I just raise my hand in confirmation when Aunt Margie walks into the room, letting it flop right back down to the cushions. I'm pretty sure the smell she's referring to is a leftover slice of pizza my dad put in the microwave for ten minutes because he's useless in the kitchen, but I also haven't showered in a week, so it could be either one. Thank God for paid vacation time at EdenMedia. I felt awful calling off when I haven't been working there that long, but sometimes, you just needed a mental health day. Or seven.

"She's been like that since she showed up here last week, crying and wearing nothing but a sweatshirt, and hasn't moved from the couch except to shuffle to the bathroom," my mom informs her, talking about me like I'm not even here.

Which I'm not. Mentally, at least.

"She wasn't wearing any pants?" Aunt Margie asks in shock, because of course that's what she focuses on.

Not the fact that I showed up here crying. Not the fact that I've been here for an entire week. Not the fact that I'm lying like a slug on the couch that has become my home for seven days, with greasy, frizzy, unwashed hair, because showering is pointless, still in the same sweatshirt, because even though I've been hurt by the man whom it belongs to, and who shall remain nameless, his sweatshirt still smells like him, and I can't deny how good he smells, even if he broke my heart.

I pull the neck of it up to my nose and take a big whiff, dry heaving a little and immediately pulling it back down. Well, it *did* smell good. Now it smells a little bit like cheese. At least I'm wearing pants now. A pair of my dad's sweatpants that are two sizes too big for me, but whatever.

"In this U.S. city, filled with stars and palm trees, it is illegal to lick a toad," Alex Trebek questions on my parents' television.

"What is Miami?" my dad shouts from his recliner in the corner of the room.

"It's L.A., Dad," I mumble from the couch sadly, feeling a sharp pain in my chest.

"What is Los Angeles?" contestant number two asks when he presses his button, the answer confirmed by good old Mr. Trebek, which makes my dad grumble in annoyance.

I only know that stupid, useless fact, because the man who shall remain nameless spent an evening googling random, stupid facts about the city he grew up in and reading them out loud to me, while I scrolled through the channels on his television, trying to find something for us to watch.

All of a sudden, my mom marches across the room, snatches the remote out of my dad's hand, aims it at the TV, and turns it off.

"Hey! I was watching that!" my dad complains.

"We're gonna miss the first Daily Double, Mom," I add, my voice a little muffled since I pulled the blanket up over half my face, with just my eyes peeking out.

"No more Jeopardy, no more Wheel of Fortune, and no more lying around on the couch smelling like last week's cheesy bacon hotdish, feeling sorry for yourself."

"Why do *I* have to suffer just because *she* doesn't feel like showering?" my dad complains, crossing his arms with a huff.

"Henry, go out in the garage and fix something," Mom says with a roll of her eyes.

With some more grumbling, Dad pushes himself up from the recliner and stomps out of the living room. When he's gone, my mom walks over and sits on the edge of the coffee table right in front of me. Aunt Margie lifts up my blanket-covered feet from the end of the couch, scooching under them and flopping down, placing my feet in her lap.

"Talk to us, sweetie. I know something happened between you and Brent. Just tell me what it is and I'll fix it," Mom says softly.

"Don't say his name. His name is dumb and I never want to hear it again."

"Fine. Tell me what happened with your *neighbor*," she amends. "I can't fix it if you don't tell me what the problem is."

I let out a huge sigh, knowing she won't stop pestering me until I tell her everything. I should be thankful she hasn't bugged me before now. As soon as I walked into the house last week with red and puffy eyes, she made up a bed for me on the couch, kissed me on the cheek, and never once asked what was wrong. She knew I needed time, and she gave it to me. But now my time is up.

I push myself up into a sitting position on the couch, letting the blanket fall from my shoulders as I pull my legs off Aunt Margie's lap and hug them to my chest. I spend the next few minutes telling them everything.

After a week of crying non-stop, I thought my tears were dried up, but I was wrong. They come pouring out of me again when I recount everything *that man* said to me in his bedroom, how he listened to my podcasts without telling me, and how our entire relationship was one big lie. I leave out the part about how I had to turn my cell phone off because he wouldn't stop calling and texting me, telling me he was sorry over and over, asking me if I was okay, and begging me to tell him where I was just so he could make sure I was safe. I don't need them to know each and every one of those texts and voicemails almost made me waiver and go running back to him. They don't need to know how weak he makes me, even though I'm sure they can obviously see it right now.

"So he basically only went out with me because he felt sorry for me, and now I don't ever want to see him again. I think I'll probably have Dad go pack up my house, and I'll just live here forever and never trust anyone ever again, because all men are liars," I finish dramatically, swiping the tears off my cheeks with the back of my hand.

Mom and Aunt Margie are quiet for several minutes, and I almost start to worry about what they could possibly be planning to do to get revenge on the guy who shall not be named. I mean, this is Minnesota, and the meanest thing they would ever do is not apologize for bumping into his shoulder if they ran into him in public, but still. They would be *thinking* a lot of bad things about him, so there's that. It makes me feel better than I have in seven days imagining all the bad things they're thinking about him right now.

"So what you're saying is, he listened to all your recordings?" Aunt Margie finally asks.

"Yes, my podcasts," I confirm with a sharp nod.

"The podcasts that are all on your website thingy?" Mom questions.

I nod again, almost feeling like I could smile if I put

some real effort into it that my family gets me and totally understands where I'm coming from.

"The podcasts that are, you know, available to the public, for *anyone* to listen to, that you don't have a fancy password or lock or something protecting? How dare he listen to something thousands of other people have listened to," Aunt Margie states.

My eyes narrow as I glare at her.

"I thought you were on my side?"

Aunt Margie shrugs. "I am. But I also think you're being a tad overly dramatic."

I turn to look at my mom, hoping she isn't going to be a traitor as well.

"I love you, Heidi, but I have to agree with my sister. Did you even hear *anything* Brent said to you? He's proud of you. He loves you. And he didn't listen to those things to hurt you. It sounds like he listened to them to better understand you, because you were still trying to find your voice and didn't know how to tell him those things at the time," she explains softly. "While I agree you have a right to be a little mad and a little hurt that he didn't tell you he listened to them, you also never told him you were recording all those things, talking about *him*, for everyone to listen to. In the last few weeks, I've been stopped by I don't know how many people telling me they listened to your recordings. Oh, sure, you never mentioned him by name, but anyone in this town who listened to them and knows you knows who your neighbor is."

For the first time since we broke up, I start to feel a little guilty at what she's saying. I too have been stopped at random places like the grocery store by someone who wants to tell me they listened to my podcast, and that even though my language was a little too colorful, they still enjoyed what I had to say and loved listening to my transformation from shy, quiet, weird girl to strong, confident, sexy woman, who is still a little weird but owns it now instead of trying to change myself.

It's not like I knew my podcast would blow up and thousands of people would be listening to it week after week. But once it did, I never stopped talking about *him*. I never thought about his privacy or how it might make him feel that people he might know would be listening to it. People in a town where he's still considered the new guy, where not everyone has gotten to know him like I have and don't really know what kind of person he is. Sure, I said a lot of great things about him, but I also complained about him not making a move on me. I made him sound like a giant… pussy who didn't know how to please a woman.

Oh, God! I made him sound like a giant pussy, and he didn't even get mad at me about that!

He never once got mad, or accused me of making him look bad, or told me to delete the podcasts. He told me he was proud of me. He told me I amazed him. He told me he didn't admit he listened to them, because he didn't want to ruin what I was trying to do for myself.

He let me take charge, because I needed to do it for myself, and he knew that. If he had asked me out like he wanted to when he first met me, if he would have led our entire relationship from the start, it never would have helped me. I would have just let him make all the decisions and make all the moves without even giving it a second thought, because it would have just been easier and it's what I've always done. And nothing would have changed. I wouldn't have realized I *do* have a voice, and I *do* have confidence, and I *can* be sexy and courageous. I never would have fallen in love with him, because he would have been like every other guy I dated—someone who didn't understand me at all.

"Did your mom ever tell you the story about Grandma Larson and how she met your grandfather?" Aunt Margie asks.

I shake my head back and forth and sniffle loudly.

"Oh, I just love this story, ever since Peggy first told it to me years and years ago," Aunt Margie says. "Well, your grandmother threw herself a twentieth birthday party and invited a few friends over to your great-grandparents' house," Aunt Margie starts. "She'd gone on a few dates with your grandfather, but she wanted to play a little hard to get, so she ignored him for a few weeks after their previous date and was waiting for him to come to her. But she still made sure he knew he was invited to the party by telling *her* friends, who told *his* friends. Well, your grandfather showed up to your great-grandparents' house with none other than Dirty Neck Bertha "

My mom laughs and shakes her head.

"Oh jeez, I forgot all about Dirty Neck Bertha!"

"Do I even want to know about this Dirty Neck Bertha person?" I ask.

"She was the town floozy," Mom says, taking over the story from my aunt. "She got her name, because she liked to do a lot of necking in the back of cars with a lot of boys she wasn't going steady with. Anyway, your grandmother flipped her lid when Dirty Neck Bertha walked into her party on the arm of the man she really liked, but didn't want to let on how much she really liked, and also never told the man in question how much she liked him, even though *he'd* made his feelings known on their first date. Well, one thing led to another. There was a lot of shouting, a punch bowl got knocked over, your grandmother told your grandfather he had a lot of nerve dating someone else when she was pretty much in love with him, and your grandfather was in complete shock, because he just assumed she wanted nothing to do with him, what with the whole ignoring him for weeks thing and never saying one word when he basically told her from the get-go how much he liked her. Anyhoo, Dirty Neck Bertha went home with Dirty Hands Dan—who got his name because he worked as a mechanic in town, not because he did dirty things with his hands, mind you—and your grandmother and grandfather were married three months later."

Mom lets out a breath when she finishes the story, and I just sit here staring at her.

"Why aren't you saying anything?" Aunt Margie finally asks.

"What exactly am I supposed to say to that?"

"Oh I don't know. A thank you would be nice, considering we just helped you with all your problems," my mom says.

"How in the hell does that help me?" I shout.

"Language!" my dad yells from the kitchen.

"Go back out to the garage, Henry! This doesn't concern you!" Aunt Margie shouts back.

We hear his footsteps stomping across the kitchen floor and then the slam of the back door.

"Your grandfather might have married Dirty Neck Bertha, all because your grandmother didn't talk to him. Never told him how she felt. Was never *honest* with him. Never *listened* to him when he told her how much he liked her and enjoyed her company when they went on their dates," Aunt Margie explains. "You might not even be here right now because of that. Or you would be, but you would have grown up calling your grandmother *Dirty Neck Grandma,* instead of Grandma Larson."

"That would have been really unfortunate, especially on Grandparent's Day, when grandparents get to go to school and have lunch with their grandkids and are presented those adorable little cards their grandkids make for them," Mom says. "Do you remember the one year you made Grandma Larson a card that read, *'Grandma Larson is the best grandma in the whole wide world!'?* Imagine the phone call I would have received from the principal if you wrote, *'Dirty Neck Grandma is kind of okay, but also a floozy.'"*

My head drops down to my knees that I'm still hugging to my chest, and I wonder what it's like for daughters who have normal families. But I do get what they're saying now, sort of.

I should have listened to Brent that day in his bedroom. I should have *heard* all the things he was telling me, instead of shutting him out and assuming the worst about him.

Feeling my mom's hand on my arm, I lift my head to look at her.

"I'm sorry, Heidi. I think this might all be my fault."

"How in the world is any of this *your* fault? I'm the one who screwed all this up."

"Have I ever told you just how easy of a child you were growing up?" she asks. "I'm sure I have. I used to brag to anyone who would listen. My friends would go on and on about how trying it was to have a teenager, when their kids would get moody and defy them and be all mouthy and argumentative or completely shut down. And I'd think to myself, *Heidi's not like that. Heidi's so sweet, and shy, and agreeable, and just so easy.* And I let you continue growing up like that, never realizing I might be doing you more harm than good. I shielded you from the bad and uncomfortable stuff. I fixed all of your problems before they could even turn into problems, just so you never had to feel an ounce of pain. I never spoke to you about important things like boys, or sex, or relationships, and I never taught you how to be strong, and confident, and brave, because I just figured, I'm your mom. No one will ever hurt you as long as I'm around, and even if they do, it will be fine, because I'll fix it and make it all better. The first thing I did when I started this conversation with you after I turned off Jeopardy was ask you to tell me what was wrong, and then told you I'll fix it. By not giving you a chance to get hurt, by not letting you figure out how to fix things on your own, I never gave you a chance to find your voice. I never let you see you could be strong, and confident, and brave. I think I did you a big disservice, Heidi."

She pauses for a minute to clear her throat, and I have to swallow back even more tears at seeing my mom so emotional and guilty for the first time in my life.

"Yes, you've found your voice, and you've grown into the strongest woman I've ever known, and aside from all the dirty talk on your podcast things, I couldn't be prouder of you. But, you did all of this recently, when you should have been doing it all along. I should have been *teaching you* how to do it all this time, instead of being so thankful that you were so easy," she tells me sadly. "Life isn't easy. It's hard. And things will hurt you.

And people will disappoint you and make you cry. And when the first boy comes along who truly understands you and loves everything about you, and you think he's broken your heart, you haven't had enough practice yet to be strong and not let it crush you. You haven't been living in this thick skin of yours long enough to stay and fight for what you want, instead of running away. And I'm so sorry for that, Heidi. I'm so sorry I never taught you how to stay and fight."

Before I can let out a pitiful wailing cry at everything my mom just said to me, Aunt Margie does it for me.

"Uff da, Peggy, why'd you have to go and say all those things?" she cries loudly, sniffling and wiping away her tears. "Harold and I are going to bingo tonight at the American Legion, and now I'm gonna have to redo my makeup."

Letting my feet drop to the ground, I lean forward and quickly wrap my arms around my mom's shoulders, squeezing her as tightly as I can.

"It's okay, Mom," I whisper as she wraps her arms around my waist and starts rocking us gently from side to side. "You have nothing to be sorry for. You're the best mom in the world, and you gave me the absolute *best* childhood. Maybe we never talked about sex or relationships, and maybe you never taught me how to throw a punch if someone is mean to me, but I'm a good person because of *you*. I'm kind, and I'm polite, and I'm understanding, and I'm loyal, because you taught me to be all those things. And those are pretty good things if you ask me."

She raised me the only way she knew how. She raised me the same way her mother raised *her*, and there's nothing wrong with that. She's crying even harder now, and I don't like it one bit. I love that she opened up to me, but I never, ever want to see my mom this upset or feel so horrible about something like this, so I do my best to put an end to it.

"I'm sorry I never screamed at you when I was a teenager, or slammed my door, or ignored you for days at a time. If it will help, I will get up from this couch right now, storm down the hall, and slam my old bedroom door *twice*. I can even dramatically shout, '*Oh my God, you're ruining my life!*' if it will make you feel better."

My mom's body shakes with laughter until I'm laughing right along with her and we're both crying, laughing messes.

Aunt Margie scoots closer to me on the couch, and in between her sniffles and loud weeping, she wraps her arms around both of us.

"Oh this is just such a beautiful, beautiful moment. I love your cousins Harold, Jr., Robby, and Benjamin, but we never have beautiful moments like these," Aunt Margie complains, hugging me and my mom so hard at this point that my face is smushed into the side of my mom's, and I couldn't speak now if I tried. "As soon as I get home, I'm going to call the boys and we're going to talk. We're going to talk about women, and we're going to talk about sex, and it's going to be beautiful!"

Oh I'm sure Harold, Jr., Robby, and Benjamin, who are all in their late twenties, will be just delighted to talk about sex with their mother, all because of me. I'm going to have to do a lot of apologizing at our next family get-together.

"Are you three finished with all that blubbering? *CSI Miami* will be on in five minutes, and I want my living room back," my dad announces from the doorway.

The three of us pull apart, and when my dad is confident we're finished with all our *blubbering*, he walks into the room and flops back down on his recliner. Pushing up from the couch, I start to head toward the hallway.

"Aren't you going to watch *CSI* with me?" he asks.

I pause in the doorway, looking back at him over my shoulder before glancing at my mom.

"Nope, not tonight. I'm going to take a shower and think about a way to fix my problems."

My mom tilts her head to the side and gives me a loving smile, pressing her hand over her heart.

"Robby, it's mom," Aunt Margie speaks, holding her cell phone up to her ear. "We never talked about what you should do when your fern stands at attention and it won't go down. It's natural, and it happens to every man, and you shouldn't be ashamed. Robby? Hello, Robby? Uff da, stop screaming so I can finish explaining this to you!"

Chapter 30

"*A*ND I THINK that just about covers everything," I speak into my microphone, finishing up episode ten of my podcast and glancing down at the timer on my audio file. "Wow, that took me three hours. I hope you guys didn't get too bored. I was going to edit out my mother lecturing me about not serving you guys a tater tot hotdish or a cheeseball, and assuming this was a live radio show where she could answer listener questions when they called in, but I think I'll keep it. It is part of my life, after all. Anyway, this is Heidi's Discount Erotica, signing off."

Clicking my mouse to end the recording, I quickly switch over to my website and upload it without bothering to listen to it or edit it. It's raw and it's real and it's messy and it's me, and I'm not about to edit myself.

"Wow, that was exciting watching you do that!" my mom tells me, getting up from my couch where she made herself comfortable a little after hour one and coming over to kiss the top of my head. "I guess this means you haven't spoken to Brent since you came back home."

I shake my head at her as I close the lid to my laptop and remove my headphones to set them on the table.

When I left my parents' house yesterday and came back home, I did it as late as possible, when I knew Brent would already be asleep. I had no idea what to say to him, and I just needed to be alone, in my own home, to give me time to think about what I wanted to say. I'm not going to lie; I was a little sad he didn't notice I was home and immediately come over here, but I only have myself to blame for that. I ran away. I shut him out. I didn't respond to any of his texts or phone calls. And if I want to continue being the strong, confident woman I've become, *I* need to go to *him*.

"I have to go back to work tomorrow. As soon as I get that out of the way and catch up on everything I've missed, I'm going to talk to him," I tell her.

Thankfully, EdenMedia gave me two weeks' vacation right from the start, and they were super nice when I called in last week and told them I needed to use one week immediately for a family emergency. I felt bad about lying to them, but I didn't really feel like explaining to them I needed to take a week off because I was a heartbroken wuss who screwed up the best thing that's ever happened to her.

"I didn't want to tell you this when you were staying with us, but Brent called me almost every day checking up on you," my mom admits.

My lip quivers when she says this, and once again, I feel like the biggest fool in the world. Every part of me wants to race over to his house right now, beg him to forgive me, and ask him if we can start over, but it's not that easy. I just blasted *all* our business all over the internet once again without talking to him about it, because it's what I needed to do for *myself*. This whole journey I've been on started with me wanting to do whatever it took to be confident and happy for *me*, not to please anyone else. Brent is a big part of that journey, so I couldn't just not talk about him and everything between us. He didn't get mad about what I'd already revealed about him, but I don't really know how he's going to take it that I just spent three hours pouring out every single teeny tiny detail between us. I hope he understands I needed this outlet to work through everything in my head. And my heart.

While my mother listened. Now my mother knows more about my sex life than any mother should ever know about her daughter. But hey, we can just consider it making up for lost time, since we never had the sex talk while I was growing up.

Maybe Brent won't even listen to it. He hasn't sent me a text or called my phone since I left my parents' house. Maybe I waited too long. Maybe using my podcast as a way to reach him and apologize was immature, but I couldn't come up with any other idea that was... *me*. I can be immature. And I can reveal too much information to complete strangers. I once spent fifteen minutes telling a woman in line at the ice cream shop that I was fidgeting so much because I had poison ivy on my vagina (although I said *hoo-ha* at the time), because I was camping with my family and had to use the woods as a bathroom.

My mom gives me a hug goodbye and tells me she'll call me tomorrow. After she leaves, I spend entirely too long staring dejectedly out my front window over at Brent's house before finally turning off all my lights, locking my door, and going to bed.

Wearing his sweatshirt that I washed three times as soon as I got home. It still doesn't smell like him anymore, but at least it no longer smells like cheese.

"OH, HEY THERE, Heidi! It's good to have you back! Hope everything's okay with your family," Dave tells me when I walk into EdenMedia the next morning, shoving my purse into my bottom drawer and firing up my computer.

"You betcha! Everything's great; thanks for asking," I tell him, trying not to feel too guilty for making him think something was wrong with my family while I was out.

"Before you get too comfortable there, could you go back to studio four and see if they need anything? Got someone important recording something in there, and I haven't had a chance to check on them in a while," Dave says. "I'll watch the phones for ya."

Trading places with Dave, I quickly head down the hallway and quietly push open the door to studio four, my eyes immediately going to the small table against the wall where Dave keeps his beverages and snacks. Without looking into the big window above the DAW, and trying to make myself as small and quiet as possible so I don't disturb the recording on the other side of the window, I walk over to the table and start gathering all the used paper plates, napkins, and dirty Styrofoam coffee cups in my arms, wanting to get rid of this mess before I see if whoever's recording needs anything.

"And I'm sitting there on my couch, with my dick in my hand, completely enjoying myself and all the dirty thoughts I was having about my adorable neighbor, when my mother just waltzed right into my house."

The paper plates, napkins, and dirty Styrofoam cups fall out of my arms and flutter to my feet when I not only hear a voice I recognize coming from the speaker mounted on the wall, but a story I recognize as well. My head whips around, and sure enough, there's Brent sitting on a stool, right next to Aubrey inside the booth.

"Oh, you poor thing. How did you ever recover?" Aubrey asks with a laugh.

"I don't know that I ever have, Aubrey." He laughs back, neither one of them looking up or noticing that

I'm in the room.

Wondering what in the hell is going on, and with butterflies swarming around in my stomach as I get my first look at Brent in over a week, I quickly drop down to the ground on my hands and knees so I can calm my racing heart and figure out what in the world he's doing here, talking to Aubrey in a studio.

"All right. On to your next most embarrassing moment. And for everyone out there listening to this, I think we're up to number three. Is that correct?" Aubrey asks Brent.

"Sadly, that's correct. Lucky for you and your first ever podcast, your readers will be happy to know I have a ton more embarrassing moments to share," Brent informs her.

Aubrey is recording a podcast? Brent is telling all of his embarrassing stories for her podcast? What in the hell is happening right now?

I stay perfectly still on the floor of the studio on my hands and knees, listening to Brent tell Aubrey, and I guess all her readers, his most embarrassing stories.

He tells her about a time at his bank job, when a really annoying co-worker came up to his cubicle, and he quickly put his cell phone to his ear so he wouldn't have to talk to the guy, and the cell phone rang in his hand.

He tells her about the first time he kissed a girl in seventh grade, and how he chewed some minty gum before he kissed her so his breath would be fresh, but forgot to take the gum out. He managed to transfer the gum to her mouth and she started choking on it, and he had to call 9-1-1 and have them talk him through doing the Heimlich maneuver on her.

He tells her about the night he thought he lost his virginity, but that it turned out he didn't *really* lose his virginity. He explains that he was going to town, thinking he was awesome and doing everything perfectly, and didn't realize until he was finished that he never even put it in. He was just thrusting his penis into the bed between her legs.

Then, he tells her about the night he *really* lost his virginity, when he only lasted one pump, and then started crying and apologizing to the girl for being so bad at it.

On and on his stories go, each one more embarrassing than the last, until I realize I've been down here on the floor for almost an hour.

"Oh, Brent. I don't know whether to give you a hug or thank you for giving me the best material ever for my first podcast," Aubrey tells him with a laugh. "Really quick before we end this, why don't you tell everyone why you decided to humiliate yourself in the best way possible today."

There's a pause from inside the booth, and I take that moment to slowly inch myself up from the ground until I'm just on my knees, craning my neck to try to see over the DAW and inside the booth. Using the office chair on wheels next to the desk to rest my hand on and push myself up even more, I'm finally able to see a little bit of Brent's face.

God, I've missed him.

He looks like he hasn't slept in a week. There's stubble all over his face, his hair is a mess, and he just looks... sad.

"I messed up," Brent says quietly. "I betrayed the woman I love's trust. I made her think that everything between us was a lie, because I wasn't honest with her from the beginning. I made her doubt everything she's done and everything she's accomplished recently. I made her think I was just doing what she wanted, instead of doing everything I needed, as an ass-backward way of trying to help her. I want her to know nothing I said or did with her was ever a lie. What we had was the most honest, real thing I've ever felt in my life. I just want her to be happy. And if that's not with me, it will kill me, but it'll be okay, as long as I know she's happy. She's an incredible, smart, beautiful, strong woman, and I hope she never forgets that. She may think she didn't do it all on her own, but she did. I was just along for the ride. And goddammit, what an amazing fucking ride it was."

Aubrey closes out the podcast, thanking Brent and thanking her readers for listening, and as my body shakes with quiet sobs, the force of them shoves the stupid office chair on wheels right out from under my hand. I go flying sideways as the chair crashes into the wall, and

I land in a heap on my side with a loud "Son of a bitch!"

The door to the booth flies open, and I look up from the floor to find Aubrey and Brent standing in the doorway, staring down at me with equal looks of surprise on their faces.

"Jesus! Are you okay?" Brent asks, rushing over and dropping down on his knees next to me.

His hand runs over the top of my head before brushing some of the hair out of my eyes with the tips of his fingers. Then he touches my cheek, my shoulder, my arm, and does a quick inspection of the rest of my body, making sure I didn't hurt myself.

Once he's satisfied there's nothing injured but my pride, he grabs my hands and helps me stand up.

"I'll just give you two some privacy," Aubrey says, winking at me over Brent's shoulder as she walks behind him and leaves the studio, letting the door close with a soft *click*.

"I can't believe you're here," I whisper once she's gone.

Brent squeezes my hands that he still holds in his as we stand facing each other.

"Where else would I be?" He shrugs with a sheepish look on his face. "You wouldn't talk to me. And I didn't want to just show up on your doorstep as soon as you got back from your parents' house, because then you would know I was watching out my front window and knew exactly when you got home, and that would just be kind of stalkerish. But now I realize showing up at your work unannounced might be a little bit creepy as well."

I laugh through my tears and shake my head at him.

"I can't believe you... told Aubrey all of those things," I say in awe, nodding in the direction of the booth. "And all of her readers. You know she has like, hundreds of thousands of them, right?"

Brent lets go of one of my hands to press his palm against my cheek.

"I didn't know what else to do. It almost broke me knowing I made you feel embarrassed or humiliated because of what I did. I never want you to feel that way, especially because of something I did. So I thought the best way to make up for that was to completely humiliate myself."

He starts softly rubbing his thumb back and forth against my cheek, and I close my eyes for a minute and press my cheek harder into his hand. After not being this close to him and not feeling his hands on me in over a week, I just want to enjoy every second of this moment. But I know I can't afford to do that. Not until I tell him what I need to.

Opening my eyes, I look up at him.

"I'm sorry I ran away from you. I'm sorry I didn't believe all of those things you said to me. I should have stayed and fought. I promise, if you still want to be with me after all this, I'll never leave again. I will stay, and I will listen, and I will fight, because you're worth fighting for. And because I don't want to make a mistake like my grandfather almost did with Dirty Neck Bertha, and because I don't want to call our son up when he's twenty-seven to talk to him about erections for the first time, and I don't want our daughter to spend a week smelling like cheese."

Brent doesn't even look at me like I'm crazy.

"Noted," he says. "We'll discuss erections with our son at an age-appropriate time, and make sure our daughter showers regularly."

How in the world did I get so lucky? And how could I be so stupid to almost throw all of this away?

"I'm also sorry that I may or may not have told our entire story in every single detail for my podcast," I add with a wince.

"I know." He laughs. "I listened. Wait, is it too soon for that? Is there a certain statute of limitations where I'm not supposed to remind you of stupid shit I did?"

I shake my head at him with a smile. "No. I'm glad you listened. Now you *really* know how crazy I am. Also, did you really lose your virginity to a Serta Plush twin size bed?" I ask, trying my hardest not to smile.

"It was a full size, thank you very much. And I'm still wounded by the fact that it never called me back. I gave that thing some of my best work. It cuts me deep, Heidi. It cuts me deep."

I throw my head back and laugh.

"I just have one question," I say when the laughter

subsides. "If you liked me from the moment you met me, why didn't you ever ask me out?"

"Not to sound like a complete middle school wuss, but I didn't think you liked me back. And then when I heard your podcast and found out how you felt, I almost yanked my earbuds out and came running over to your house. But then I kept listening. And you said you were lost. I couldn't be the one who made you disappear completely because I took charge and made all the decisions. You needed to figure it out on your own. I couldn't just hand you Brent Miller on a silver platter." He gives me a wink.

"God, you're ridiculous. And I love you so much," I tell him, not at all shocked that I let it fly right out of my mouth without any hesitation or nerves.

He deserves to know. After what he just put himself through, and after what I'm sure Aubrey's readers will put him through once she uploads that thing, he definitely deserves it.

A groan of relief comes out of Brent's mouth before his arms are suddenly around me and he's yanking me against his chest. I wrap my arms around his shoulders and bury my head into the side of his neck, breathing him in for the first time in far too long as he kisses the top of my head.

"I love you too, Heidi Larson," he whispers as I lift my face from his neck, push up on my toes, and give him a *real* kiss.

A kiss I've been dreaming about for a week. A kiss better than any kiss we've ever shared before, because everything is finally out in the open—the good, the bad, and the embarrassing.

We break apart a few minutes later, and Brent laces his fingers through mine as we walk out of the studio.

"You know, you're going to have to change the name of Heidi's Discount Erotica now," Brent tells me as we walk hand-in-hand down the hallway.

"Why's that?" I ask.

"Babe, there's nothing *discount* about you. You are top shelf, premium, expensive erotica."

I roll my eyes at him good-naturedly as we get out into the reception area.

Huh. Heidi's Top Shelf Erotica. That does have a nice ring to it.

Epilogue

Heidi's Top Shelf Erotica, Episode 62

"**W**ELCOME TO HEIDI'S Top Shelf Erotica, brought to you by the Pleasure Palace, making all your erotic fantasies come true, with sex toys of every shape and size to fit every need you could possibly imagine.

"You guys, I know Heidi's Top Shelf Erotica has been syndicated for a few months now, but it's still crazy to me that I actually have sponsors!

"Okay, onto the good stuff.

"First and foremost, my honeymoon two weeks ago was amazing. Better than I ever could have imagined. Brent and I spent a relaxing and, dare I say, absolutely erotic time in Bali.

"We went to our first nude beach, and don't worry, I'll tell you all about that on next week's podcast when my special guest is here—Elizabeth Franklin, the author of one of my recent favorite erotic romances, *Take My*

Breath Away. She'll be reading an excerpt from her book that is H-O-T, hot, folks! I don't want to give too much away, but it involves a threesome on—you guessed it—a nude beach! And no, Brent and I did not participate in a threesome. We may or may not have had sex on a beach while we were there, but if we did, I promise you, it was just the two of us, late at night, and the beach was empty.

"Did everyone watch the Golden Globes last week? Did you see our boy Jameson take home the win for Best Performance by an Actor in a Motion Picture—Drama? Jameson, if you're listening, I know I already told you this on the phone, but I'm so proud of you!

"I had a lot of listener questions after my last podcast, wanting to know how my mom is. She wanted me to tell you thank you for all of your concern and kind words. She's doing fine. Her hip was not, in fact, broken, and if anyone wants the sex swing she thought was a good idea to try out, let me know and I'll send it to you. Please, I beg you, let me send it to someone. There is no way she should have had my dad install that thing in their home, and it needs to go immediately before she thinks she should give it another try.

"Let's see, what else? Oh! My good friends at my former employer, EdenMedia, sent me a new box of advanced copies of upcoming audiobooks while I was on my honeymoon. As you guys know, I partnered up with all of the publishing houses that EdenMedia produces books for. Not only do I get audiobooks, but they're also nice enough to send me paperback copies to add to my ever-growing erotic romance bookshelf in our living room. And bedroom. And spare bedroom. And a new shelf we added to the kitchen last month. And you can be darn sure I've highlighted each and every one of my favorite erotic scenes that I read for you guys. Brent likes to call them my lady spank bank.

"Anyway, I'm sorry I haven't had a chance to listen to any of them yet and find my favorite scenes to highlight in the paperbacks. I've been busy. Having lots and lots of sex with my gorgeous husband. I promise I'll start on them tonight, and I'll have my first raving review and hot excerpt ready to go for you next week, after my interview with Miss Franklin.

"Today's Top Shelf Erotic Question of the Week comes from Shauna in Michigan. Shauna writes, *'I've been struggling with finding a way to tell my boyfriend that he's just not hitting the right spot, if you know what I mean. He tries so hard, and I just feel so bad that I pretend like he's doing it right and I'm enjoying what he's doing, when I'm really not. Heidi, please help!'*

"Well, Shauna, I'm going to be blunt with you. The first thing you need to do is practice saying the words you need to say. Your boyfriend can't find your clit, am I right? And if he can't find your clit, he is never going to give you any pleasure, which leads to you faking orgasms, and that's not helping anyone, especially him. You need to be honest with him. It's going to be tough, and it will probably hurt his feelings a little, but he'll get over it. If he loves you, he's going to want to do whatever he can to please you. No more faking it. Talk to him. Help your man find your clit, Shauna! Also, check your email. I'm going to send you a 50% off coupon for the Pleasure Palace, just in case.

"Don't forget to send in your questions to me at Erotic Heidi at gmail dot com. Everyone who gets their question read on one of my podcasts wins an audio copy of whatever erotic romance I'm featuring that week!

"Also, don't forget to check out Penelope Sharp's upcoming book, *Claiming His Mistress*, which will be out a week from today. In case you missed it, check out Episode 56, where I read an excerpt while Penelope was in town for her bridesmaid dress fitting and I forced her to do an interview. This particularly delicious excerpt had some light bondage in it that will make you wet in all the right places, and it had a surprisingly funny ending to the seriously erotic scene that involves the heroine's parents stopping by. That might sound familiar to some of my older listeners, and Brent, honey, I'm still sorry about that, and I love you!

"This is Heidi Miller signing off, and remember:

You are strong, you are confident, and you are sexy as hell.

Learn it, live it, love it, and say it out loud to yourself in the mirror until you believe it."

The End

Check out all of Tara's books: www.tarasivec.com
Connect with Andi: facebook.com/VOAndi

Acknowledgments

Thank you to everyone at Audible who had a hand in helping us bring Heidi to life, as well as our amazing agent, Kimberly Brower.

Thank you, and a big sloppy kiss to Lauren Blakely for being the genius behind our title, "Heidi's Guide to Four Letter Words". Thank you for keeping us out of the dirty dungeon.

Thank you to Andi's narrator sorority sisters, who were there the night Heidi was "born" at RT: Amy Landon, Xe Sands, and Christa Lewis.

Thank you to Jennifer L. Armentrout, and everyone at Apollycon18, who allowed Heidi to make her first public appearance at the audiobook panel.

Thank you, and great big hugs to Karen and Kyle at Audio Ruckus for being the best "Daves" we ever could have had.

A special thank you to Rose Hilliard and Melissa Bendixen at Audible for all their energy, enthusiasm and hard work, and for taking such great care of us.

Last, but not least, thank you to all the listeners and readers, for your continued support, and especially for allowing us to collaborate on this story for you!